MINE

A KILLER'S LOVE SERIES BOOK ONE

JENNIFER IVY

This is a work of fiction.

Edited by editing4Indies

Cover Designed by Cormar Covers

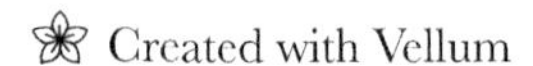

Dedication

This book wouldn't be written if I hadn't been encouraged to follow my dreams, so thank you to the two people that always have my back.
I Love you

For the readers like me, that see red flags as green… enjoy ;)

TRIGGER WARNINGS

This book is a Dark romance, and as such may contain subject matters, content, or events that you may find disturbing.

This includes but is not limited to;

Dubious Consent (Dubcon)

Blood

Gore

Kidnapping

Forced Proximity

Spanking

Figging

Rimming

Spitting

Graphic descriptions of Violence, Torture, and Murder.

A KILLER'S LOVE SERIES BOOK ONE

JENNIFER IVY

CHAPTER ONE

Charlie

"I've gotta pee so bad," I whine, wiggling in my seat.

A finger pokes the back of my head where it lays against the headrest.

"You're such a fucking child," Jason huffs. "This is the second time you've needed to go during an eight-hour ride. You have the bladder of a twelve-year-old girl."

"No." I glare at him over my shoulder. "I have the bladder of a twenty-year-old who drank four cups of coffee to stay awake all night because her roommates insisted on continuing a tradition we've had every year during college of being exhausted on our first day of vacation." Now, I'm the one huffing.

I'm too tired to bite my tongue with him.

A finger pokes at my head again. Smiling, I turn

and capture it with my forefinger, squinting my eyes as I pull the digit gently. "Remind me again why we are doing this at Halloween?"

"Because we all got busy over the summer. You worked, Laura worked, I vacationed, and we all suck." Amy smiles back. "This is the only weekend we could get together. But we did it!" Amy squeals, wiggling our fingers. "We are officially seniors! One more year and we'll be ready to enter the real world."

"If you pass and can get a job," Jason mumbles.

"You know, you're a great boyfriend. I'm always telling Amy how supportive you are," I snark.

"Come here," he tells Amy, pulling her close with an arm wrapped around her shoulders and leaving his hand hanging dangerously close to her chest. "I just don't want you to get your hopes up and then fail." Placated, she cuddles into his side. "Besides, it's not like Laura isn't just gonna get a job at her daddy's company after she's finished bumming around Europe. But you were right, you do suck." He winks.

Gross.

Seeing my face, he grins. "And I'm always telling Amy if you were less sarcastic and put out more, you wouldn't be single." The sole of his foot connects with my seat. "Maybe if you jump on Dale's dick, you'd be less of a bitch," he says, nodding at his friend beside me.

"And maybe if you had a bigger dick, you'd be less of a prick," I whisper.

Another kick to my seat says he heard me.

"Kick the seat again, and we won't have to stop!" I warn him. My bladder really is full. "And for the record, Laura worked really hard at summer camp. You'd know that if you hadn't spent most of the time harassing the female counselors and getting high with the local loser." I attack back. Meeting Laura's gaze in the rearview mirror, I see how his comments stabbed at her insecurity. And the bitch in me lashes out again. "Don't be bitter just because your daddy skipped out on you."

The look he sends me gives me chills.

"Ignore him, babe. He's just playing." Dale's heavy hand squeezes my knee. "Don't worry if you get scared. You can bunk with me." He winks.

I push his hand off my knee, giving a small smile to soften the blow. "I think I'll be okay."

I'm not interested. I wasn't a week ago when this was a girls-only trip, and I'm still not, even if my roommates have turned this into a couples trip.

Well, two couples plus Dale and me.

"You didn't really flirt with the women there, did you, baby?" Amy asks in a small voice.

"You know I didn't. I was too busy calling you whenever I was free," he placates.

"I wish I could have been there." She sulks.

"I know, me too, but you just didn't apply early enough. I showed you how much I missed you when I got home, though, didn't I?"

Gag!

"Besides, if I hadn't worked at the camp, we

wouldn't have somewhere to stay on this little trip." He jangles the cabin keys.

"Tell me again how you managed to get the keys?" Now I'm pouting. "I barely saw you working all summer."

He smirks, and Amy answers for him. "Because he's charming and has never met a woman who can say no to him."

"Delila was our camp supervisor and is sixty-five. Somehow, I don't think she's falling for his charm, and besides . . ." Turning more, I look him dead in the eye. "No," I say sternly. "There, now he has," I tell Amy.

The car pulls to the right.

Oh, thank God.

Laura turns into the parking lot of a gas station, stopping next to one of only two gas pumps.

"Go, go. Babe, out." Jason ushers Amy out of the car before it can even come to a complete stop.

"Hey!" Laura yells after them. "Watch the damn door! It nearly hit the pump."

"I'm sure your daddy would just buy you a new one," Jason calls back over his shoulder, not caring about the door they left gaping open.

"Not the point," she mumbles from the driver's seat.

When they reach the door beneath the *Ladies* sign, he turns back. "Charlie, find somewhere else to pee! This is occupied." He winks.

Confused, I watch how he grabs his crotch before

smacking Amy on the ass and following her into the toilets.

My eyes widen in realization. *No!*

They can go get nasty in the woods. It's not like a thick forest doesn't surround us. I will not pee behind a tree!

Not for that asshole.

Shuffling forward in my seat, I dig my hand into the pocket of my jeans and fish out ten dollars. Reaching my arm over, I tap Laura on the shoulder before dropping the money into her lap. "I know we said twenty dollars each, but my purse is in my bag, and I've really, really got to pee, like now. I'll give you the rest after." Getting out, I close the door before shutting the one behind mine with my hip.

Laura's laughter is drowned out behind the metal as it closes.

As I jog past the gas pumps to get across the parking lot, the blare of a horn startles me, ripping a loud scream from my chest.

My body reacts on its own. My right leg bends up as my hip turns away, and my right arm moves to shield my face.

I stand there like that for a second before I realize . . . I'm not dead.

No pain, no impact.

Lowering my arm, I peek over my hand and stare wide-eyed at the large pick-up and the huge man driving it.

Air whooshes out of me at the same time I realize just how close the truck is.

Millimeters.

I almost died.

Because of Jason.

What. A. Dick.

Trying to steady my heart, I straighten up before rushing around to the driver.

"I'm really sorry, sir. Are you okay?" My breath catches in my throat when I see the two men in the truck's cab more clearly.

The driver says something—just one word—but I can't see him properly to tell. He's probably cursing me out, but then he turns, only to glare at me through the closed window. I do what I always do when I'm nervous . . . I ramble. "Please don't be mad. I really am sorry. They're having sex, and I really need to pee."

He gazes toward the end of the building where I pointed before returning the same pissed-off eyes back to me. My soul shrivels at how much of a moron I sound. "I just need to pee," I say again, the words barely loud enough to be heard.

I hold my breath as he lowers his window. My gaze flicks to the passenger, who I think is angry, too, if his flushed face is anything to go by, before I look back at the furious driver. I track his movement as his tanned arm extends to wave me closer.

"Stay," he demands, pointing at the ground beside his door. His voice makes my body shiver. And I don't seem to be the only one shocked by his demand because his passenger's head swivels from me to the big guy driving so fast that I think it might roll off.

But I only look at him for a fraction of a second because the growly driver has my whole focus. At this moment, he's my world, but my body has locked in panic, and I'm as still as a statue. The need to obey is so strong my mind goes blank.

When I don't move, he snaps his fingers and points at the ground again.

This time, my feet move of their own accord, and I obey him without thought. The back of his hand brushes my stomach after his raised brow tells me to shuffle forward a little more.

A firm nod tells me I am where he wants before he slowly drives past the pumps and parks.

As soon as his harsh gaze is out of sight, my body quickly reminds me why I was in a rush.

A pain shoots through my bladder.

Crap.

My brain kicks in and tells me I can't just stand here in the middle of a gas station parking lot because some super-handsome, flannel-wearing mountain man orders me to.

Wiggling, I shift, turning my body toward the bathroom. My foot lifts off the ground just as his truck door slams closed.

My head snaps toward him, and my pulse races again when he quickly approaches. The sound of his boots hitting the asphalt pulses through me. The look on his face forces my bottom lip between my teeth, but the act does nothing to hide my quivering chin. For the second time within a few minutes, I'm questioning what the hell I'm doing.

Feet glued to the ground, I'm rooted in place as he storms toward me. My body is caught between arousal and fear.

A pounding pulse settles between my legs and my body has decided.

It takes everything in me to swallow the whimper that rises when his strong fingers steady my chin. His skin burns as hot as his gaze. His eyes roam over the front of my body like a caress of his hands until they lock on my chest, where my beaded nipples have hardened with arousal.

He doesn't say a word as our gaze meets. His green eyes hold me captive, and I simply stand there as he crowds even closer.

The feel of his boot kicking my foot back a step to where it had been startles me, causing me to jerk back. He is quick to steady me. His hands span my waist, his fingers touching the middle of my back.

I have never felt so tiny and safe yet scared. Every fiber of my being screams he's dangerous, but those same parts of me want him.

My senses are as confused as my body—like something bad will happen, but I'll enjoy every minute of it.

My whole body is alight. Energy hums under my skin where he touches me, and my skin tingles where his thumbs brush back and forth just below my breasts.

"Hey! Get the fuck away from my girl."

Dale's voice startles us both.

The big guy blinks down at me and shakes his head like he's trying to clear it, telling me I'm not the only one pulled into their own world.

The hands on my waist tighten enough to make me gasp.

I can hear Dale rushing toward us, but as I try to twist and look behind me, the mountain of a man in front of me takes a giant step to the right, spinning us in place to put himself firmly between Dale and me.

His hands remain where they are. They're no longer teasing but now feel as harsh as his gaze looks. "I said stay," he reaffirms, staring me down.

"Hey! I told you to get away from her."

Still hidden behind a mound of muscle, I can only hear Dale. I don't realize how close he is until the sound of flesh hitting something hard reaches my ears.

It takes a second for my brain to register that the sound and the slight movement in the mystery man's shoulder are not separate events.

Dale hit him!

In the back! *Coward.*

I feel my jaw drop before instinct takes over. "What the hell are you doing?" I demand, trying to move around the man between us and confront the jackass.

I don't get far.

The hands on my waist slide to my hips, holding me in place.

Struggling, I push to my tiptoes and glare at Dale.

If looks could kill, he'd be so dead!

A firm squeeze to my hips has me dropping back down, my feet firmly on the asphalt.

Really? I silently ask.

Hoping my expression conveys my thoughts, I try to round my truck driver again. This time, instead of squeezing his hands in warning, I feel a sharp swat to my jeans-clad ass.

I'm not sure if the pain or the shock stops me in my tracks—maybe both—but I stare wide-eyed at the gorgeous stranger who just spanked me in the middle of a gas station parking lot.

"You do not listen well, little one. That will change." His voice is hoarse, like he just woke up or spent the past decade smoking thirty a day.

His words lodge my breath in my throat. *What do I even say to that?*

"Go," he tells me, nodding behind me.

I can't get my legs to move because my brain is too busy processing what just happened.

"Toilet," he says, pushing at my hip.

It's the jolt my body needs to wake up, and my legs carry me in the direction he pointed without much thought.

Before I even reach the bathroom, both curiosity and intrigue tell me to turn and check on Dale. Yet every fiber of my body and my instinct scream at me to keep walking and not stop until I'm inside the restroom.

Curiosity wins.

Maybe I was a cat in a past life?

But it doesn't matter. I shouldn't have bothered. By the time I turn to look, Dale is rushing back to the car, diving into our middle row of seats like his ass is on fire and slamming the door just as Laura and Billy climb out of the front seats.

The truck's passenger and my mystery spanker watch Dale with identical expressions of disgust. Like he's a bug they want to step on.

A thought I do not get to dwell on before I am once more locked in a heated gaze. A battle of wills I'm not sure I can or want to win.

CHAPTER TWO

Daniel

Cockroach.

I watch as the boy scuttles back to the car, hiding as if some rich city boy's car will be able to keep him safe.

The thought of holding him by the neck with his head in the doorjamb of the car as I slam the door over and over makes me smile. But it only lasts a second when the appearance of his friends from the front of the car reminds me that I need to reel my urges in.

At least until tonight.

Stepping away, I hope the physical distance will help tear my mind away from what I could be doing. I glance down at what touches my foot. A pumpkin.

They are placed around the gas pumps as a reminder of what today is.

Halloween.

When all the monsters come out to play, including me.

The thought of what is to come sends a shiver down my spine and makes my cock swell.

I close my eyes and let my body feel the excitement, the anticipation.

It's not just the night itself I enjoy. It's the build. October is a month of foreplay.

So much so that even the sight of a pumpkin, the smell of cheap candy, and the taste of candy corn—all things I associate with this time of year—get my dick going.

Because they mean Halloween is close. The one day I can stop holding back and get to be myself. And what is more arousing than that?

It's been ten years since we did it the first time. And each kill since has only gotten better.

I eye the car, letting my imagination run wild; their fear, their pain. The screams and the blood.

My cock twitches.

But there's only one problem. Turning, I look at it. Look at her.

Really look. Because for the first time, I wonder what it would feel like to sink my body into a woman. Not any woman, just her.

Little girl needs to learn to do as she's told, I think when

I see that she has not only stopped but turned to watch.

Probably worried for her pissant boyfriend.

The idea that she's his has me marching toward her, and I let my anger show. All thoughts of my brother forgotten as I leave him standing there.

I watch as her dainty throat swallows. She's scared. *Good.*

My steps don't falter, not even as she quickly backs up. We reach the door to the ladies' room at the same time, only she has turned to push her way in.

Her hand touches the door just as the wood bangs against the frame, and something slams against it on the inside.

My girl jumps, startled, and her back bumps into me. I know the instant she feels the hardness of my cock against her back because her body arches and tries to move away.

I wrap my hand around her throat. She's not going anywhere. Her chin brushes the back of my hand, and I draw her back flush with my body.

A feeling she'll need to get used to.

The door bangs again, and I realize it's not something but someone hitting it on the other side when a loud female moan quickly follows the second bang.

Her friends are fucking against the door.

At the sound of what's happening behind the closed door, the woman pressed against me melts into me more.

Her body wants me, needs me. Not that it matters, though, to make her mine.

"Crap," she cusses.

When she tries to pull away a second time, I tighten my hand around her neck. It is no longer a pressure on her beautiful skin but a restriction. A warning.

"Please," she whimpers. Squeezing her legs together, she wiggles her hips slightly. The friction against my body does nothing but make my cock harder.

But it reminds me of why she rushed out in front of my truck. Eyeing the door next to the one in front of us, labeled *MEN*, I reluctantly release her.

She quickly takes a step forward, turning to face me.

A frown pulls at her plump lips, drawing my attention there.

She's upset, and my mind takes me to all of the things that I could do to see this look again. Only next time, I will have caused it.

But my mind can't do it. I want more from her than her fear.

I want her lips swollen and red as I forcefully shove my fat cock down her throat. I want her lips to quiver as I fuck her and refuse release until she tells me she loves me. And more than anything, I want to watch as her tears roll over those plump lips and hear her cries drown out my moans as I fuck my seed into her.

My body hums. I don't think I have ever wanted anything so badly.

Not even my first kill.

For the first time in my twenty-eight years, not only do I desire a woman but I want her enough that I have zoned out. Too caught up in fantasizing about our future and what I will do to her that I don't even notice her moving.

Something that will never happen again. I fucking know better! Always be aware.

This is how you get killed. I should know.

My annoyance shows on my face, a sneer taking over. But my girl is too far gone in her own irritation to notice the danger she's in.

"Urgh." She stomps her foot. It's cute.

Cute? What the fuck is wrong with me?

Disbelief and a little disgust run through me. I want to fuck a woman more than I want to kill her. I'm normally content to fuck my fist as I wash off the evidence of my crimes, so I don't know what to do with her. All I know is that I don't want this to end yet.

I don't want her to leave my side.

"I really, really didn't want to have to pee in the woods. Are there bears here?" she asks, looking panicked. "Am I gonna have to pee with a giant freaking bear watching me?" She doesn't wait for a response, instead only continues to wind herself up more. "A big, giant, pervy bear. All because I insulted Jason when he was being mean, and now, he needs to get his dick wet to prove a point. Like why?" she asks but doesn't wait for an answer. "I already know he's a giant asshole."

The angrier she gets, the more her arms flail. Her body rotates between facing me and the woods. Seeing her perfect ass wrapped in tight jeans reminds me of how she felt pressed against me.

When I start to imagine pinning her arms behind her back, bending her over and fucking her in full view of her precious boyfriend, I pull myself together.

Taking a steadying deep breath, I take the few steps needed to walk around her and push the men's toilet door open.

Holding the door, I nod at her to go inside, to which she scrunches up her face.

Fucking adorable.

And because I both detest and am not used to speaking, I bark, "Inside, little one." Needing to see how far I can push her, I say, "No bear gets to watch you pee." As she passes me, I add, "Except me," and wink at her when she pauses.

Her face tells me she's not sure if I'm joking, and her beaded nipples tell me she's not sure whether she wants me to be serious.

But I rarely joke. Another thing she'll get used to.

Giving her ass a sharp slap, I encourage her to enter the bathroom and close the door behind us. The overhead lights flicker as I shut out the bright winter sun. And because I meant what I said, I press my back against the door to stop anyone else from coming in.

She stands in front of me wringing her hands, unsure what to do.

"You have needed to use the bathroom since you almost dented my truck. So I suggest you place your cute ass on that toilet before I decide you need help with going." My throat screams at me, pain shooting through it with every word.

Once she has decided I'm not bluffing, or at the very least doesn't wish to find out, she turns and scurries toward one of the stalls on our left before quickly coming straight back out.

She must hear me sigh because she spins to face me, pointing back at the stall. "That. Is disgusting. I would rather give Goldilocks and the bears a free show."

I fight a smile as she goes into the middle stall.

Again, she exits quickly. "Why is there no door? What exactly do men do in here?"

I don't even try to hide my smile at that, nor do I offer an answer because I don't have one.

She barely reaches the door at the third stall before gagging and backing up until she hits the sink. Gripping the edge of the porcelain behind her, my girl considers her options.

Biting her lip, she turns to me, and I can see the tears in her eyes even from here. The sight is as beautiful as I had hoped.

"I really, really need to pee," she whispers.

I frown at her squirming and nod to the middle stall. "So pee."

All movement from her stops, including her breathing. Her whole body freezes.

I watch transfixed as her mind and body fight. She doesn't know it yet, but it doesn't matter which one wins.

Nothing can stop what's coming.

She seems to sense this, or maybe she really just can't hold it anymore, but with tentative steps that turn more and more determined, she walks into the middle stall.

My eyes drift to the mirrors above the sink, opposite the stalls, giving me a perfect view to see her lose some of the bravado.

"Hey, mister?" she calls. "Sir?" She tries again when I don't respond.

"Daniel," I tell her, "but I think we'll keep the sir." I smirk at her through the mirror.

"Could you turn around?" she asks. Clearing her throat, she tries again in a sterner voice. "Don't watch, okay?" Again, I remain silent, so she adds in a small voice, "Please, sir."

And those words do something to me that I never thought I would feel, that I could feel.

I turn away to the left, leaning my shoulder against the door. Not because she asked me—I'll watch her whether she likes it or not—I turn because I don't want her to see me.

I can hear her fiddling with her pants and lift my head.

The smirk that takes over my face is feral. There's another mirror.

It's small, and it sits above a lone sink in the space between the wall I lean on and the stalls. But I don't need it to be big, I just need it to be exactly where it is.

It's perfect. I can see the room, including the other mirrors behind me directly in front of the stalls.

I take everything in; the way she anxiously bites her lip, the way she has to shimmy her hips because her jeans cling to her body, the way her pussy looks with the patch of soft brown hair above it, the way her thighs tense when she squats over the toilet seat while her face scrunches in disgust of having to use that stall.

I can't get enough of any of it.

I watch her captivated.

"Can you say something? I don't want you to hear me pee." Silence is the only answer she receives. "Daniel?" Again, I don't answer, and instead watch as a frown takes over her pretty face. "Are you still there? Sir?" She whispers the last word like she's afraid of what will happen when she uses it.

"Hmm," I grunt, wanting to show her that the use of the title pleases me.

Understanding that she isn't going to get what she wants, she starts to hum. The sound does nothing to cover the noise of her urination, and she knows it.

A blush spreads over her cheeks, disappearing down into her yellow sweater. My fingers twitch with the need to strip it off her and see how far down the blush goes.

So focused on her skin, I miss as she wipes between her legs. Expecting her to pull her pants up and exit the stall, I watch in surprise and fascination as my girl straightens, reaches out and takes more tissue paper.

Wadding it up, she grasps hold of her panties and dabs at the inside.

Confused, my head tilts as I watch until it clicks, and my whole body straightens.

Her panties are wet!

"Did you pee?" I snap, my tone harsh.

I need to know. Because if she didn't, I want it acknowledged aloud that her pussy wept for me. That she craves my dick as much as I crave burying it inside her.

"You know I did," she bites back. "We both heard it, but thank you for making this so much more humiliating!"

One day very soon, I will smack that sass right out of her with my hand on her bare ass.

"Tone!" I reprimand sharply. "Did you piss yourself, girl? Or did you wet your panties for me?"

Her head snaps up at my words, our eyes meeting through the two mirrors.

Even from this angle, I see her eyes well with tears and her lips tremble.

"You watched?" she breathes. The statement sounds more like a question as disbelief fills her face.

The look is quickly followed by outrage.

She takes one last swipe at the material, balls up the now damp tissue, and tosses it into the toilet.

She straightens fully again, and because the mirror is directly in front of her, or maybe it's that she can feel my gaze eating up every inch of her, her hard gaze finds mine again. Her expression tells me she can't believe I'm still watching.

I am not bashful.

"You can glare all you want, little one, it won't change shit," I tell her.

I watch as she pulls her panties up, hiding herself from me. Her jeans quickly follow.

"It will if I kick you in the nuts," she mumbles under her breath, but the words are spelled out for me as I watch her lips move.

Sassy. I smirk. *Something that will need to be trained out of her sooner rather than later.*

She takes a moment to close her eyes and take a deep breath, probably to gather more patience as my little one looks ready to blow.

But it doesn't matter because, like I told her, it won't change shit. Nothing will. She could throw the world's biggest tantrum, and the only thing it will do is make my cock harder as I imagine doling out her punishment.

Nothing and no one can stop what's happening between us, nor what will come.

Stepping up to the sinks, she reaches out and squirts some soap out of the dispenser into her hands.

"At least they have soap in here." She's talking to herself, trying to defuse the tension. Her body screams her discomfort. "I didn't think men washed their hands."

My lips twitch with the need to poke at her. "They don't . . . That's why there's plenty left," I tease her, something that is foreign to me. I'm glad I did, as the smile she gives me is blinding. Her cheeks dimple as her mouth spreads wide, and a small chuckle escapes her.

And for that one second, she looks at me like I'm normal. The way she'd look at anyone else she was interested in. Maybe even the little dickhead outside.

Seconds later, our moods sour.

Hers, because her mind reminds her that she is supposed to fight this, and mine, because I want to kill her boyfriend now, not later.

Clearing her throat, she says, "I should go," with a nod to the door behind me.

I stare as she tosses the used paper towel in the bin, and with her head down, she walks toward me with hesitant steps. No, not toward me. My sweet girl thinks she can make it to the door behind me without getting too close.

And because I like to play with my prey, that's exactly what I do.

I tilt my head and watch her; the way her eyes peek at me right before she takes her next step, the pause she does after taking said step, and the way she takes a deep breath as she passes me. Because despite being scared, she feels the need to take some part of me inside her, even if it is just my smell.

And the thrill that gives me is like nothing I've ever felt before.

I turn my head to keep her in view, my body frozen until her small hand touches the door. I spring toward her, my hand slamming against the wood of the door, forcing it closed.

"What . . ." The words get lodged in her throat. "What are you doing?"

I wish I could see her face as I crowd closer with my arm braced above her. "Your friends might not be finished yet."

She shrugs. "I'll wait in the car."

With the boyfriend?

"I don't want you seeing anything." It's a weak reason to keep her in here, and she knows it.

"It's gone quiet," she whispers over her shoulder, looking at my chest.

With a finger under her chin, I lift her face until she meets my gaze. "I guess it didn't take him long." I smirk.

"I wouldn't know," she whispers, with a small shrug.

A blush spreads over her cheeks, and her gaze darts around the room, anywhere but me.

What is she saying? That she's never slept with him, or that she's never slept with anyone?

My hand is around her throat before she can blink, her back now pressed against the door.

Our breaths mix as we each wait to see what the other will do.

"Charlie," she breathes, her lips grazing mine.

My tongue wets my lips instinctively, touching hers as it does.

"What?" I ask through my foggy brain.

"That's my name . . . Charlie," she explains. "Charlotte, actually. But my friends call me Charlie." My girl likes to ramble. Silence bothers her. "You never asked me . . . what my name is," she whispers, her tongue peeking out to wet her lips, and she brushes mine this time.

"It doesn't matter," I tell her, crowding in closer. Caging her in with my arms, I watch her shiver as my words and their meaning roll over her. "I'll be calling you mine."

My lips press against hers, but I don't know how to do this. With a growl, I keep my lips on her skin and move to her neck, my tongue tasting her.

Her small hands clutch at my shirt but quickly move to shove my stomach as hard as she can when I sink my teeth into her neck.

My moan fills the small room. I finally get the taste I've wanted since I looked at her.

Her blood touches my tongue; her taste fills my mouth.

Need burns its way through my body.

Desperate.

I'm desperate to sink my cock into her. To force her to take me.

A solid bang on the door startles us both. Another first for me.

I step back, ready to defend us, except Charlotte moves with me. She turns in my arms to face the door. Her hand joins mine on her throat, as if my firm grip comforts or maybe even makes her feel safe.

I stare down at the crown of her head in amazement. Everything about this woman is made for me.

Anger mixes with arousal.

"Come on, Charlie, enough sucking his cock! That's what I brought Dale for," a male voice yells, followed by a foot connecting with the door.

Charlie jumps again. Someone will die—and painfully—for giving my girl that look of fear.

"Shhh," I soothe, caressing my thumb back and forth over her pulse point. "No one will harm you, ever." I feel her relax in my arms and choose to press her, prepare her. "Except me." I growl, sinking my teeth into her shoulder through her sweater.

And although it does not excite me the same as when I could taste her skin, the soft panicked cry she gives, with the rapid rise and fall of her chest, along with the feel of her breast resting against my forearm is just as good.

"Please," she begs.

What for, I don't think even she knows. Her fingers pry at my hand while her ass pushes back into my cock.

"That word will not hold much weight with me, good girl." I grind into her as my words register and tighten my hand just enough for her panic to set in. "Go," I tell her, releasing my hold. "Have fun with your friends. Enjoy Halloween."

Her back remains plastered to me, even after my hand no longer holds her. I take in the feeling of her choosing me, even if only for a second. Then I push her hips and land a solid smack to her ass.

It's enough to get her moving.

Charlotte opens the door just enough to slide through and looks back at me one last time. Her eyes hold the question of what happens next.

"Because this will be the best one we ever have . . . by far," I say to the empty room.

It takes me a few minutes to calm down enough to exit the bathroom. I'm so hard I even consider taking care of my problem here in this shitty bathroom.

As soon as I exit, I see Charlotte in the middle row of the car with that little fucker. I take pleasure in knowing he'll be the first one I kill tonight.

The other kid comes out of the building with a grin as he rushes to the car.

"Go! Go! Go!" he shouts.

The driver, a pretty petite brunette, panics and skids out of the lot once he's closed the back door. Young men shouting and cheering trail out of the open windows.

Charlotte's panicked face looks out of the side window, searching for me. She turns in her seat and mouths, "Sorry," through the back window.

I walk a few steps quickly, not understanding what

happened. Until Duke, the gas station owner, steps up beside me.

"Little shit said his friend was going to pay. That's sixty bucks of gas and another ten on food they had that I'll never see."

"You okay to clean Daniel's truck?" Michael asks.

Duke nods, still looking after the kids' SUV.

Blindly, I reach into my jacket pocket and pull out six twenty-dollar bills. Folding them, I pass them over.

"I couldn't," he resists.

"Your family has been around almost as long as mine. We take care of each other in the town, remember?" my brother tells him with a hard look, spewing the same shit my parents have been saying all my life . . . well, most of my life.

"Thank you, kid." He nods at me, taking the money, and being the good townfolk he is, Duke doesn't point out that Michael and I are not true Cromwells. Not by blood at least.

But it's not blood that matters around here. It's money. And that, we do have.

"Someone needs to teach those kids a good lesson," he mutters before walking off toward my truck.

"I think we can manage that, brother, don't you?" Michael smirks. I don't answer. I never do. Not since that night . . . until her.

I needed her to hear me, to do as I order. My voice sounds weird, like it doesn't belong to me. No longer the voice of a pleading child, it's deep and rough. Growly from years of no use.

Michael watches me, perhaps hoping for a verbal response. Instead, I nod once before pointing at the road where the car has now disappeared before pointing at my chest.

As always, my brother understands. "I know. I saw." A laugh huffs out of his chest as he claps me on the shoulder. "I heard." He swallows down his emotion before continuing. "She's gonna fight it, but if you want her, we'll make it happen."

I nod again. *I do want her.*

I have never asked for anything, only that my brother be safe. I did that, so I can do this.

I give Duke a few minutes to get started before heading his way to take over. I'm not about to watch a seventy-year-old man struggle to wash my truck, not when I'm more than capable.

That's not the type of torture or humiliation I enjoy.

CHAPTER THREE

Charlie

I love my friends, I love my friends, I love my friends. I repeat the mantra over and over in my head.

Hunched over, leaning on the kitchen island, I dig the heel of my hand into my eyes.

Heaving a sigh, I try to gather what's left of my patience. "What do you mean we can't turn the lights on?" With a quick lift of my head, I glare at Jason. "You said we had permission to be here!"

"No." He grins, throwing the keys onto the counter. "I said I got us the keys."

"No one gave you the keys, did they?" I clarify.

"Give, take." He shrugs. "It's all the same thing."

"Yeah . . . no, no, it's not." *Fucking moron.*

"Oh my God, I'm going to get arrested," Laura gasps. "I cannot get a criminal record. Do you know how bad that would look? Oh, hi I'm Laura your new accounts manager and an actual felon!" she screeches, slapping her hand on the old wooden kitchen top.

Jason and Billy laugh, which only seems to set her panic off more.

Very quickly, she starts gasping for air and having a full-on panic attack.

I send Amy a look that says I think she's an idiot for dating him, only to receive a sheepish smile.

I don't know what she sees in him, but I also don't bother asking because I know the answer. The same one she always gives . . . *He's good in bed.* I roll my eyes. *Oh please, no one is that good, right?*

"Baby, breathe," Billy encourages, trying to coach her to mimic his own breathing. She's not having a fucking baby.

I swear to God, where do they find these boys?

Stepping around the counter, I gesture to Amy to give me a hand with Laura. We're used to helping her manage the anxiety that comes with disappointing her parents.

"Deep breath in," Amy ordered, "and hold."

"Good, Laura, you're doing great," I encourage.

"And out. And in."

Once I see Amy has everything under control, I turn to the fuckup and his number one fan.

Pointing my finger at Billy, I glare. "You're supposed to be her boyfriend. How about you do something other than laugh at his lame ass before you find yourself single?" I gesture toward Jason.

Suitably reprimanded, Billy steps closer to Laura, tugging her into his embrace. I don't hear the words he whispers to her, but I watch as her body relaxes fully, and she tucks herself into his arms more firmly.

I look around the kitchen counters, and when I don't see what I'm looking for, I start opening drawers.

By the sixth empty drawer, I slam it closed in frustration. "There have to be candles or flashlights around here somewhere. You can't tell me this camp was full of kids a few months ago, and they didn't leave anything behind."

"Lost and found." Jason pipes up.

Huh . . . I guess he does have a good thought every now and then.

"Try not to break any more laws while you're looking," Amy teases him. She winks at Laura, who has now completely settled.

"What? It's not like she'd have to worry anyway; her daddy would just make it go away for her."

Bewildered, I just stare at him. He really can't help himself.

Unable to take much more right now, I head toward the front door. "I'm gonna go unload the car."

"I'll help." Dale volunteers.

"No! Dude, I need you to help me check out the bunk cabins."

Apparently, that's all the convincing he needs because Dale and Jason leave through the back door. They turn left, the opposite way to the kids cabins.

"Let's go claim a room." Billy winks at Laura.

"Gross," Amy mutters, scrunching her face at me.

"That's all I see with you four, all day, every day," I tell her, wiggling my finger back and forth between Laura's and Billy's retreating backs. The smile on my face tells her I don't really mind.

Laughing, Amy follows me out to the car. "You love us."

"I do." I nod. "It's the only way I'd put up with Jason."

"I know." She nods. "I think I'm going to break up with him," she whispers.

"I'm sorry," I tell her, but I'm not really. Good riddance. The man really is an asshole.

Amy shrugs. "Plus, I can get good sex elsewhere."

Fair.

Dropping the last bag into the cabin doorway, I nod toward the car.

"Think Laura will mind if I borrow her car?"

"Oh yeah. Like slept through her alarm on the day her parents are visiting kind of mind."

A laugh slips out before I can stop it. "We shouldn't laugh," I tell Amy when her giggle joins mine. "She was genuinely a nervous wreck."

"That's because her dad has a stick constantly stuck up his ass."

"True." I nod.

"Why? Where are you going?"

Stepping backward off the wooden porch, I point

my thumb behind me. "I'm going back to pay for the gas."

"It'll take you like an hour to walk that!"

"Probably." I grimace. "But I won't sleep tonight if I don't make this right."

"Here." Reaching into her pocket, Amy hands me twenty bucks. "I'll halve it with you when we head back Sunday?"

"Thanks." I appreciate it.

Smiling, I head back toward the main road, which sits at the end of the dirt tracks running through the camp.

CHAPTER FOUR

Daniel

We are headed to the family cabin to meet up with everyone else after helping Duke clean my truck when I see her.

The little shit is walking along the side of the road with her back toward the oncoming traffic.

Anyone could take her!

I press on the brake, slowing the truck as we pass her to get a better look. She doesn't even lift her head!

Anger rolls through me like never before.

My palm itches, the kind that only the feel of her reddened skin can cure. A solid spanking would certainly gain her attention.

Loosening my grip on the steering wheel, I use it as a scratching post, scrubbing my palm against it.

I'm torn about what to do. Tonight, that'll be easy.

Natural. But this? It goes against everything I have ever felt.

The sight of her small frame in my side mirror is all it takes.

I barely look at Michael before pulling sharply on the wheel, sending us into a quick U-turn.

His booming laughter fills the cab of my truck. I ignore him, along with the need to punch him in the throat.

I appreciate him not actually saying anything. Still . . . asshole.

Oblivious, Charlotte keeps walking. I swear to God, this girl.

Walking along the dirt between the wide road and the trees, Charlotte does not hear us approach until I accelerate and merge onto the dirt path, heading straight for her.

I watch as she spins, a startled look making her big doe eyes pop wide, her mouth dropping open in fright.

My cock swells.

I don't stop the truck until it's between her and the forest, placing her at my door. The sudden stop of the wheels sends puffs of dirt around the truck bed.

Shoving the door open, I simply glare.

Her Converses shuffle back and forth, scratching at the dirt. She meekly looks at the ground, peeking at me every few seconds as if to check if I'm still mad.

I am. With every fiber of my being.

But I know it's not all directed at her. I'm the one

who turned the truck around. I'm the one whose mind has locked itself on a target of a whole new kind.

Taking a steadying breath, I point at the ground next to me.

Charlotte reacts instantly.

She's a natural at taking orders.

Once she has stopped in the small gap of my open door, I mimic my earlier action from our first meeting and click before pointing at the spot I want her in more harshly.

Her bottom lip disappears into her mouth, but she doesn't argue and shuffles closer.

Her stomach is firm and flat beneath the back of my hand, which I leave pressed against her as I move it up and over her body.

Her sweater rises with my hand, baring a sliver of her tummy. By the time I get between her breasts, we're both panting.

Her eyes flutter closed, and her lip pops out of her mouth, wet and inviting. A gasp shoots out of her tempting lips when my hand snaps around and takes hold of her neck.

I can't take much more than this. I have never needed anyone like this.

I tighten my hand more, but Charlotte still won't look at me. The tighter I go, the more she squeezes her eyes closed.

Her body shakes, but her pebbled nipples tell me she's just as aroused as I am, as do her tightly pressed thighs and flared nostrils. But I choose to focus on the former.

Releasing her neck, I trail my forefinger over her pulse point until I reach the end of her chin. Tilting it back, I tap the little dip in her chin with my thumb until her eyes finally open.

Bright and light. The color has paled, somehow becoming lighter with her arousal.

Charlotte tilts to her left slightly and gives Michael a little smile and a small wave. My rage builds. I have never, ever felt violence toward my brother before this girl. I could not have imagined it, but right now, I want to stab him in the neck with my truck keys.

I don't get to dwell on my dark thoughts for long because when Charlotte looks back at me, she gives me the brightest smile anyone has ever sent my way.

My heart expands in my chest. Is it possible to love someone with one look?

I twirl my finger in front of her face, only for her to do the cutest fucking spin that ends with her still facing me.

I make a sound that I don't think I've ever made before. I laugh. It's deep and rough, but it's definitely a laugh.

This woman.

I feel my brother's hand on the back of my neck. The squeeze a silent acknowledgment of what just happened.

My heart fills my chest even more. It feels as

though it wants to reach out and absorb her into my body.

To make us one.

So that's exactly what I do.

Reaching out with both hands, I firmly grip her shoulders and turn her. A thought occurs to me to be gentle, but that wouldn't be me. And I need someone to see the real me for the first time in my life.

My large hands grip her underarms, and without warning, I lift her clean off the ground and right into my lap.

Just as I settle her onto my thighs, she tries to slide farther back and off onto the bench seat.

I am having none of it.

My arm is a wall of muscle as it hooks around her waist, my hand spanning her stomach to slide her ass back onto my thigh.

At first, she struggles, but when my pinkie finger slips under the waistband of her jeans, brushing her lace panties, Charlotte quickly uses my knee and shoulder to situate herself more comfortably on my right leg.

The need to make sure she doesn't sit comfortably for days nags at me, but I push it aside. No doubt my girl will earn herself another spanking very soon.

I settle my right hand on her hip and tap the underside of her shoes as a sign to lift them.

Her brow scrunches. "Please, can I just sit on the seat?"

"No."

"Daniel" — she sighs — "I'm not going to fit. I'm too big!"

"Hardly. You can barely be five feet and a hundred and twenty pounds soaking wet," Michael corrects her for me.

"Five feet two, actually," she mutters, her legs still hanging out of my truck.

"You're very petite." I can hear the grin in his tone and know he's about to deliver a blow. "Small enough that you should be praying your kids take after you and not my brother. Imagine pushing that out."

Michael's words do the trick, and when I next tap the bottom of her shoes, she lifts them automatically, not thinking, too caught out by his words.

Grabbing her ankle, I push up to bend her knee more, her body tilting slightly as I move her foot to rest on my left thigh. To steady her, my right hand releases its hold on her body and grips the steering wheel, giving her my arm to lean back on.

Once her feet are on my leg and securely out of the way, I quickly close the truck door.

No escaping now. Not that there ever was, not since that first look of fear she sent me through the windshield.

I point at the edge of the cab bench, where a small space between my thigh and the door is big enough for her dainty feet to rest.

Charlotte does as told but gives a little huff to show her displeasure.

She's not the only one uncomfortable. My cock is beyond painful. Tucked into the leg of my jeans, it fights to get out. The material of my pants is pulled as tight as it goes, and the heat of her ass on my thigh is like the target of a heat-seeking missile. With every wiggle and movement she makes, the harder it tries to get at her.

And it's obvious the minute she feels it below her. Her whole body freezes, and her big, innocent eyes find mine.

I don't try to hide my thoughts or my wants. Why bother? She can feel it underneath her now, and she will feel it inside of her later tonight anyway.

And because I have never been like this before, never wanted this before, I cannot stop myself. My hips surge up, pushing into her hard, before dropping back onto the bench.

I need to get a grip. I have always judged others for their baser needs. It makes you weak. Something Michael and I often take advantage of on our Halloween hunts.

It makes it so much easier to sneak into a house at night when people are sleeping—everyone knows that—but it is even easier to get in unnoticed when they're fucking. Too lost in each other to notice or even care what else is happening.

I never saw the appeal until now and look forward to learning about it.

But there is a time and place. Right now, I have a bad girl in need of a lesson.

Words have never been my thing. I'm rough as I shove her right knee into the steering wheel, and her left into my stomach before delivering a solid slap to her jeans-covered thigh.

The resulting crack echoes inside the truck. It sounds hard, but I know it lands even harder. I need her to feel it.

Charlotte barely gets her shocked cry out before I deliver another smack to the same spot. I want her thighs burning when I crawl between them later.

I deliver the hits quickly and succinctly.

By the third slap, her senses return, and self-preservation kicks in. Her knees knock as she clamps them closed. My hand is now stuck between them.

She needs to learn not only that she will take all punishments I choose to give but also that fighting me will only make them much worse.

Pinching the sensitive skin at the top of her thigh, I twist until she screams, pushing up on the balls of her feet, her ass lifting off my thigh. And then I twist some more.

"Down!" I bark.

And like the good submissive she is, Charlotte drops her ass back down roughly.

"Please! It hurts!" she begs, shoving at my forearm.

It seems she needs another lesson. Letting go, I watch as relief visibly passes over her face, but it doesn't last long as my fingers latch onto the skin of her other leg, giving it the same treatment.

A growl is all she needs this time when she attempts to push up again.

As she cries, her tears drop down her flushed cheeks.

Her body shakes with the force of her weeping.

I release her skin. "We'll start again," I tell her.

We all sit in silence, minutes passing with Charlotte hunched forward hugging her knees, before heaving a big breath. Her eyelashes still hold tears when she peers up at me through them.

"Please." She tries one last time.

When I give no response, a sob escapes her. And then another. They don't stop coming, not even as she opens her legs, positioning them back to how I had placed them before.

My arm, anchored on the wheel, braces the full weight of her body again as she trusts me to hold her up.

I start on her left thigh, then her right. Making sure to spank over the spot of her pinched skin every few hits.

The slaps do not lessen in force nor speed as I deliver them.

My heavy breathing, the blows to her inner thighs, and her cries are now the only sounds in the cab.

I lose track of time, but my whole hand aches when I deem Charlotte to have had enough. The fire in my palm tells me her legs are burning enough for her lesson to have sunk in.

Her hair has fallen forward to cover her face,

hiding her from me. I brush at her cheek, wiping it away where some has stuck to her tearstained skin.

"Good girl," I tell her, tucking the strands behind her ear. "My good girl."

A blush spreads over the crest of her cheeks and down her neck. I follow it with my gaze as it disappears under the yellow wool of her sweater and watch as her chest rises on a hiccuped sob.

We sit there on the side of the road as Charlotte calms herself down.

Her face now exposed, I get to watch as she bites her lip to stop it from trembling. But it's useless, and when it's set free, it instantly pouts out.

The need to taste it rises up, so I do.

Leaning forward, I duck down and suck her lip into my mouth, nipping it before soothing it with my tongue.

Happy, I go to pull back, but I'm startled by the touch of her tongue against mine.

Gasping, I pull back a little, but her mouth follows mine, fusing us just as quickly as we separate.

A groan rips out of me. One of her own joins mine when my hand tangles in her hair and pulls.

No longer supported by my arm, her body drops toward mine, her shoulder meeting my chest, and her legs fall closed.

I tear my mouth away and lay her head beneath my chin. Her small hand settles on my chest, her fingers playing with the buttons of my plaid shirt. I can feel her move her left hand from where it had landed in my lap and look down to see her slide it between her legs.

A whimper escapes her as she touches the no doubt sore inner thighs.

We sit quietly, a peace settling within myself at the feel of her in my arms, my hand running back and forth across her hip, trailing down every few passes to give her ass a good pat.

I press a kiss to her forehead, causing her body to go completely lax. At first, I think she's fallen asleep, but when I look down, I'm met with her open stare.

This girl really cannot hide her thoughts. The question of why is written all over her face.

Charlotte is apparently not the only one unable to hide her thoughts, as Michael sees I cannot answer her like I want to. Too caught in my emotions, words fail me.

"Do you have any idea what could have happened walking along the side of the road like that? With your back toward any threat?" Michael asks from behind her. "That will not happen again."

"No, sir." She quickly agrees with him, but her eyes are on me.

She understands that my brother is saying the words I cannot.

"Where are your shitty friends?"

Ignoring his question, she mumbles, "They're not shitty."

Charlotte's eyes drop from mine, only to dart back up when my hand lands harshly on her ass.

"Well, maybe Jason, but he's not a friend." She amends, adding, "Neither is Dale."

Just the mention of the boys she's traveling with gets my blood boiling. I look over at my brother on the passenger side of my truck cab and urge him to ask the question I want answered the most.

"And the third boy? Your boyfriend, what's his name?"

Charlotte frowns, shifting in my lap and trying to look over her shoulder at Michael. My short growl stops her. Only when I feel her small hand stroking at my chest do I realize I never stopped making the sound.

Leaning my head back, I close my eyes and take a deep breath. I'm not used to being out of control, and the thought forces me to take another calming breath.

Charlotte's weight slowly settles against me again. She's gentle as if afraid to hurt me, or maybe she's worried about another spanking. The why doesn't matter. I just enjoy the feeling of her weight on top of me and imagine us in other places, with other ways that I can enjoy the same feeling.

I don't know how long we sit like this, but it's long enough for Michael to have turned on the radio so a local station fills the silence. The voice of a town member by the name of Kent tells us about a deal our local Walmart has on pumpkins.

Charlotte peeks over at my brother. I can feel her forehead turn. Not completely, just enough to see him, and then it moves back.

"He's not my boyfriend," she whispers. "Jason, the dick who ran out without paying . . . Dale is his friend."

I force myself to remain still as she moves.

"Not my boyfriend," she whispers against my mouth with a gentle kiss.

"Good," I whisper back, my eyes meeting hers.

I see Michael's hand coming toward us and have to remind myself that he is my little brother. Still, my breath lodges in my throat for a second as he catches a lock of her hair, giving it a quick tug.

"Welcome to the family, little lady. I'm Michael." He smiles at me, giving Charlotte a quick wink.

With this feeling in my chest, my brother at my side, and my girl in my lap, I start my truck and pull back onto the road, doing another U-turn.

"Where?" I ask her.

"They're at the camp," she answers, telling me where her friends are. But that's not what I meant.

"Where?" I try again.

"Oh, I was going back to the gas station."

When I don't speak, she adds, "Laura and Billy are getting busy, and she's a little protective of her car. That thing's her baby . . . so I walked."

Michael's sigh is just as loud as my own.

"What?" She shrugs. "It's not like I got into a car with a stranger . . . well, until you forced me." She grins.

But I'm not laughing because what if it hadn't been me?

CHAPTER FIVE

Charlie

Is he still mad?

I don't know what to say, but I know I need to say something to fix this.

I hesitate before leaning back toward the gap between the brothers, keeping as much distance between our upper bodies as I can so that both of us can think. Clearly, that goes out the window when we're near each other. "I'm sorry." I don't know why I say it, but I do.

Nor do I know why I'm sorry, but I am.

A stranger being angry with me for walking alone shouldn't bother me, but it does. He matters, and it's why I still sit in his lap.

Like he'd let you go if you tried, my mind taunts. I push the dark thought aside quickly because no matter what kind of connection I feel, I sit in a truck with two men I know nothing about.

"I just wanted to go back and pay." I explain, "We didn't know Jason was going to do that. I'm not like that." I look back and forth between them. "Really," I insist when they don't acknowledge my previous words. "I won't be able to live with myself if I don't pay."

I need to go back, but if he drives any more, I'll be walking farther than I would have from the camp.

The burning in my thighs won't let me even think about asking them to stop and let me out to walk back, so instead, I ask him to take me back to the gas station.

"You want to go back and pay?" Michael asks.

"Yes." I nod.

"No," Daniel answers me.

Shit! My shoulders sag at his refusal.

I don't want to walk after what he did, especially knowing he might catch me. Maybe I can sneak there tomorrow?

But just the thought of upsetting him has tears filling my eyes, and my body's reaction only serves to upset me more. What the hell is wrong with me?!

Daniel looks down, catching sight of my face.

The truck stops so sharp, his tight grip around my waist is the only thing stopping me from slamming into the steering wheel.

"You're crying."

It's a statement, but he sounds confused. Like he can't understand why.

He stares down at me until my chin wobbles and a tear breaks free.

Suddenly, I find my face pressed against his chest, his hand holding me in place.

"Okay," he says, but I feel the truck turn again, heading back toward the gas station.

"Who'd have thought?" Michael asks. "Out of all the women in the world, you'd pick a good girl."

"My good girl."

I don't know if it's the words, his growly voice, or a combination of both, but it makes me melt, physically and emotionally.

And I know, without a doubt, I'm in trouble.

CHAPTER SIX

Daniel

Michael grins, shaking his head as we pull into Duke's station.

Still in my lap, Charlotte has now shifted forward, eager to get a better look out of the windshield.

Duke must have seen us approaching because he's already at my window to greet us by the time I pull up. A light blush appears on his face when he sees Charlotte sitting on my lap. A raised brow is the only indication of the questions I know must be running through his head.

"Hey Duke, Daniel's girl," Michael says, hesitating, "wanted to come back and pay."

Charlotte shifts, mistaking Michael's pause for dislike of what her friend did, but I realize . . . he doesn't know her name.

"Charlotte," I say, resting my hand on her inner thigh, an encouragement to speak up.

"Charlie," she corrects, smiling at Duke. "I'm sorry we left without paying, sir."

I twitch. The use of that title for anyone but me just doesn't sit right.

"I'm really sorry, Duke," Charlotte tells him, and she means it. I can hear it, and Duke must see it because he reaches up and pats the back of her hand where she's gripping the edge of the open window.

"I understand, dear," he reassures her. "We'll just forget about the whole thing."

"Oh no." Charlotte shakes her head.

Dropping her whole body into my chest, I hiss as she crushes my cock beneath her hips. She digs into her back pocket while giving me a cheeky grin and a quick kiss to my cheek when she pushes up off my chest.

"Sixty bucks, right?"

When no one answers her, Charlotte looks around at us. "What?" She settles her gaze back on Duke. "I thought the pump said sixty when we drove off."

"The gas was sixty, sweetheart, but he grabbed some food while inside."

"Oh." I watch as she worries her bottom lip. My hand strokes her leg when she bites down particularly hard. "I only have sixty in cash . . . well, forty, but Amy gave me twenty," she rambles. "But I have my card. I'll just come inside and pay the rest." She smiles.

Charlotte tries to open the truck door, but I keep a steady hold on her, and Duke pushes against the truck from the outside so that it closes just as quick as it opens.

"Boys," Duke starts unsure.

"Duke," I say, my voice a stern warning.

The old man doesn't know what to do. Shocked, he stands staring open-mouthed.

He's prideful and honest, so he doesn't want to take payment for something I already reimbursed him for, but the money means shit to me. If my good girl wants to pay him and keep her conscience clean, then I will make that happen.

Michael, being better both verbally and socially, speaks up, helping me to smooth the way for Charlotte. "I'll spot you the ten, good girl, and save you from having to get out. Duke," he called out to him, looking around us. "I'll bring this truck for another clean start of the week on our way back from the cabin. I'm sure it'll get filthy again from the dirt roads." When Duke remains hesitant, Michael delivers the final blow. "Charlie here walked a good distance before we picked her up. She won't feel right if she doesn't fix this herself, Duke."

Duke sighs, turning to Charlotte, whose frown quickly switches to a huge grin.

"Okay, but only if the little lady promises not to walk along this road alone again." Her smile doesn't fall, not even at his disapproval. "It's dangerous. Trucks use it to avoid some of the highways, not to mention the out-of-towners who cut through here. No one would know if anything happened to you."

Charlotte nods, contrite.

Her earlier reprimand was at the forefront of her mind, I'm sure.

My cock twitches at the idea of her thighs burning every time she moves for the next few days. I feel myself leak precum at the knowledge that after Halloween, tonight, it won't only be her thighs that scream discomfort when she moves.

"Yes, sir. I won't do that again; I definitely learned my lesson." She peers at me from under her lashes. "Who knows what kind of weirdo freak might just pluck me off the ground and into his truck."

The grin she's fighting to hold in shows she's teasing me. Something that doesn't happen often . . . never, actually.

There's that feeling again. I rub at my chest, trying to soothe it.

"Well, we can't have that, can we?" Michael agrees, handing her the extra ten she needs.

Taking the money from her outstretched hand, Duke looks between Charlotte and me.

"I, uhh." He struggles. "I didn't realize you were seeing anyone, Daniel."

I don't reply. I don't want to, nor do I need to.

After a few minutes of silence, he backs up from my truck, patting the open window. "Make sure you bring this by for another clean. Yours too, Michael."

"And I really am sorry, sir."

"You've more than made up for it," Duke reassures her.

Problem solved, I tug her back into my body before putting the truck into drive.

The drive is peaceful, something I don't feel too often. The sound of Kent's voice filtering in through the speakers as he interviews the local PTA about safety precautions the kids and their parents should be taking tonight . . . given that we had a murder of a tourist last Halloween in the very heart of our own small town.

They don't need to worry about their little ones not going out alone. They're safe whether or not they stay in groups while trick-or-treating.

No, we don't hurt children. Besides, my good girl has given me more than enough to do tonight. And who knows, maybe it'll result in our own trick-or-treater not so far in the future.

Charlotte brings me out of my thoughts. She shifts as if uncomfortable, but the look she sends the radio tells me it's the topic that makes her uneasy, not my massive erection that is desperately trying to find its way inside her.

Her body faces forward, her legs hanging on either side of mine.

"Wow, I didn't hear about any murder from the other counselors."

"Murders," Michael corrects.

"What?"

"Murders, plural. There have been a few over the

years. And a few hikers who have apparently been victims of a bear." He smirks, like the idea is ridiculous.

"Bears and murders? I'm so glad I agreed to come."

"You're in Idaho now, Charlotte. There are many scary things in these woods," Michael tells her.

He's baiting her, I think, but I growl when she tenses because while what my brother says is true, the only thing my girl needs to worry about in these woods . . . is me.

Michael gives a dark laugh. "I wouldn't worry too much. It seems you have your own bear now."

Charlotte settles back against me, and I can feel the exhaustion that flows through her. Dropping a kiss on the crown of her head, I silently give her permission to rest.

She's content to just lay here, and her body molds into mine. My right hand wanders down and rests on top of her thigh while my left lazily guides the truck, my elbow on the window ledge. And at this moment, Charlotte isn't the only one that feels content.

Returning Michael's smile, I kiss the top of her head again as we pass the turnoff for Cromwell campgrounds.

Quicker than I would like, we're turning off the side road that leads to my parents' cabin. A few miles farther, I turn onto the small, unused road that leads to the campgrounds from the back, where no one can see us since we're miles away from the main road and where none of the camp security cameras have coverage.

I don't want to wake her, but just as those thoughts pass through my mind, Charlotte moves.

She's awake. Maybe she has been the entire time. It thrills me to think she trusts me enough not to question me when she had no idea where I was driving us.

I have never cared if someone followed me without question, but now, I find her blind trust is not only something I want but need.

Reluctantly, I shove the truck door open.

"Come," I encourage, helping her slide off my lap and onto the ground.

Her earlier bravado is gone, and my shy girl is back. And this side of her is mine. With her friends, she was loud and dominant. But standing here with her gaze down, watching her restless feet, she is the submissive that I crave.

With a steady finger under her chin, I force her eyes to meet mine. "I'll come for you," I tell her. The words sound every bit of the threat they are.

Her nod is small, unconvinced.

"I'll come," I tell her again.

This time, I watch as the side of her mouth hitches up.

"You better."

I nod for her to head inside. The weather is turning. The sky has darkened, and the clouds are moving in. A thrill rolls over me again at what sounds and sights the darkness will hide tonight.

"Don't open the door to anyone tonight," Michael calls out as I start the truck. "You never know if it's a trick or a treat." He winks.

"I'm sure we can handle some kids looking for candy." She laughs off, backing toward the main cabin. "Just don't snitch to the townies that we're here."

My brother leans forward to see around me. "We are townies, Charlie."

She gives him a matching grin. "Yeah, but the cool kind, not the 'this is our town, no outsiders' sort of townies. Besides" — she blushes — "getting me arrested would make you officially the worst brother-in-law ever!"

She doesn't wait for our reaction before she turns and hightails it into the cabin. Had she stayed, she'd have been the first person to ever watch my cheeks grow hot. Instead, I had to listen to Michael tease me about how bad I have it and how she'll have me domesticated in no time.

Something we both know is neither possible nor true.

But I let Michael have his fun. It's what brothers do, right?

He doesn't knock it off until our parents' three-story lakeside home comes into view. Our home for the weekend—my mother's idea, a chance for the family to spend time together and to bond more.

"Daniel," Michael says, pulling me back, "I'm really happy you found your one." He clears his throat when the words get stuck. It's hard because we're not like this. I'm not like this.

"I have you're back like you had mine. Whatever you need," he promises.

His words mean a lot. I don't say that, though. I just give a solid nod.

"And for what it's worth, I really like her. She'll come around in the end."

This time, I don't spare him a glance when I climb out of my truck. Because although I wouldn't be able to express to him how important his opinion is, even if I could say the words, I know that I don't need to.

Not with him and apparently not with Charlotte.

I have never really thought about souls and being bound. I have just always known that I was meant to be here with Michael to protect and watch over him.

But now I know, without a doubt, that the three of us are connected.

I feel it.

Michael and Charlotte are mine, but something is missing. As I walk up the wooden stairs and past the trick-or-treat signs, I can't help but picture a few additions to the Cromwell household, a few extra souls waiting to join us.

CHAPTER SEVEN

Charlie

"Ahhh!"

The scream startles me, and I drop the red plastic cup, the contents spilling onto the counter.

Billy! The asshole.

What is it with men needing to scare the crap out of their girlfriends? Do they enjoy us wanting to cuddle after? Do they like feeling as if they saved the day, despite the fact we wouldn't need it if they didn't scare us out of our minds?

Morons . . . or maybe it's just these three because Daniel and his brother didn't seem stupid.

That's what it is: age. I tell myself I'm never dating a college boy again.

Not that I ever have. Well, not really.

At the thought of Daniel, my irritation rises. I

haven't heard anything from him all day. Of course I haven't—the man didn't even ask for my number.

I've changed my mind. It's not men, it's me.

I'm the moron.

Why did I think he'd call or come by?

Tilting my head back, I sigh. I'm disappointed and embarrassed. I let a man I don't know do . . . I don't even know what to call it. Is it spanking if he didn't touch my ass?

And in front of his brother!

"I am a moron," I groan.

"At least you're gorgeous."

Dale's voice startles me, and I spin quickly, too quickly. I'm dizzy, so my hand shoots out to catch myself on the counter before I can fall.

"Easy." He grins, his hands settling on my waist.

"I'm fine," I huff.

I am fine. He and Jason have been extra annoying since I got back. But maybe it's more to do with the annoyance I feel at myself, I silently admit.

Trying to be less of a bitch, I move out of his grasp to get a cloth. Holding the yellow material between us in explanation, I force a smile until Dale backs up enough from the counter that I can step in and clean up without him so close.

Turning toward the counter, I pick up the cup and start to soak up the whiskey and Coke.

Wrong move.

I feel his hands on me within seconds.

They're higher this time, too high.

So much for being nicer.

"You hurt my feelings earlier when you wouldn't kiss me for your dare," Dale tells me, and I feel panic rise as his body presses against the back of mine.

My mind compares the feel of him to the way Daniel felt against me. My body trembles, and not in the same way the large man made me shiver earlier today.

Dale feels it and takes it as a green light.

"I guess you just needed us to be alone." His words are spoken into the skin of my neck, where it's still sore from Daniel's earlier bite. I try to cringe away, but the final straw is the feel of his tongue wetting my neck from shoulder to ear.

I shove myself from the counter and pull away from him, but it just leaves me backed into the corner of the L-shaped counter. What little moonlight coming in from the window behind me is enough with the few candles littering the room to see the intentions in Dale's eyes change.

This is bad . . . this is really bad.

"Dale—"

"You know . . .," he interrupts, taking a step closer to me. "I've been patient. Jason said you were a tease but that you'd let me fuck you after a few drinks."

I eye the now empty cup, and the image of him following Amy into the kitchen to fetch drinks earlier flashes through my mind.

Who passed me the cup? Dale. Dale gave me both my drinks tonight.

"What did you do?" I barely get the words past my throat.

"Nothing." He laughs.

I don't believe him, and my face tells him so because he gives another laugh, his hand brushing the air as if to wave away the topic.

"What did you put in my drink, asshole?" I snap, now out of patience.

Shit, does a town this small even have a hospital?

My chest feels tight, and my breaths are getting faster, shorter. I'm having a panic attack.

"It's nothing. It was just something Jason gave me when we went out for a smoke to chill you out . . . a bit of E is stashed in the car."

A bit of E? As in ecstasy? *This fucking man!*

I take it all back. It's not me. It's most definitely all them!

I am trying to think of when he gave me the drinks. The first was early, way before they went out, as it wasn't even dark then.

I glance at the clock above the oven.

Twelve-oh-nine A.M.

So it was only in my second drink. Did I drink it?!

No! I had been about to when Laura's scream scared me.

Okay, so maybe I'll take Billy off the moron list. That just leaves Daniel, Jason, and the asshole standing in front of me.

Too lost in my own thoughts, I don't notice as Dale worms his way closer to me until it's too late.

His mouth is on mine, and his tongue is in my mouth before I can stop him.

Our bodies are so close that I can't get my hands between us to shove him off. The taste of the vodka he and the boys had been taking shots of makes me feel nauseous.

I punch at his side, but Dale only grips my face tighter.

Panicked, I do the only thing I can do. I stomp on his foot. It's not the most precise attack nor the strongest—I'm sure there is a self-defense teacher who would fail me out of their class had they seen it—but it's effective.

Dale lets out a screech that would make a dog cringe. His fingers dig into my cheek before he hops back, spitting curses at me, but . . . fuck him!

And fuck this trip!

I rush around him and out the back door, gulping as much air into my lungs as I can. I keep running, stopping only when I reach the tree line.

My heart pounds, my whole body shakes, and my chin clenches as my tears break free.

I need to make a new list for him to go on: the biggest, douchiest, moron of all morons! That's what he is.

Argh!

A sound behind startles me. When I turn, the back door is still open, but Dale is no longer in the kitchen. I glance around to check that he didn't follow me out.

He didn't.

My body sags with relief. I genuinely don't know what I would have done if he had.

Another scream rips through the air, louder this time. Traveling out of the open back door and disappearing into the woods.

It sounded like Laura.

I roll my eyes. I want to stay out here a little longer, but it's pretty cold already, and I can feel the bite of the wind more now that my body has calmed.

Is it too late to go back and kick him in the nuts?

Jackass. The more I stand thinking about it, the more riled I get.

He tried to drug me. Drug me!

What would have happened if I had drank it?

That thought makes me freeze on the spot as horror washes over me. And now I am no longer cold. I'm burning up. Pure rage courses through me.

I'm going to kill him. No, I'm going to kill them both!

I'm sure I can hide a body or two out here.

That is the last thought I have before I rush toward the cabin.

CHAPTER EIGHT

Daniel

I watch them through the small window. His fucking eyes are all over her.

A sharp nudge to my ribs distracts me.

Michael.

The fucker elbowed me!

I glare at him from the corner of my eye. Now is not the time to test me.

He holds his hands up as if surrendering before pointing back at the bushes we had been using for cover.

When I ignore him, Michael jabs his finger at the window, his own eyes, and then back toward the bushes.

They'll see us.

He's right.

I know he's right, but it doesn't stop me from wanting to get closer. I have never wanted to kill someone more.

It'll come. I reassure myself.

That thought running through my head, over and over, gives me the strength to retreat. I just need to wait a little longer.

The little cockroach might be looking, but he won't get anywhere. Not while I'm standing out here.

I settle on my haunches beside my brother. No longer standing, I'm forced to look up at them. My view is not only narrowed by the edges of my mask but it's also restricted by the window ledge.

He's moving closer, too close. She's not paying attention.

And then he's on her, hands caging her face, his mouth on hers.

Shoving my brother's hand off my shoulder, I stand with every intention of tearing that boy's hands off my girl, and then ripping them from his broken body.

I don't even make it to the house before his pain-filled wail sounds. He's stunned and practically crying.

Charlotte is barely a hundred and twenty pounds. What damage could she have possibly done? Fucking pussy.

I have already closed the distance to the house by half, too far to turn back and hide. But she doesn't see me when she rushes out of the house. Too mad, Charlotte storms past me, past Michael's hiding place, and keeps going until she stands at the tree line.

My brother takes Charlotte's obliviousness to her surroundings as a chance to slip into the house. I wait for the impending scuffle, but I guess the chickenshit ran back to his room with his tail between his legs.

I, too, slip into the kitchen. Michael has already gone farther into the house, no doubt eager as to who he will find first.

But me? I have my eye on one particular target tonight. First, I'll capture her. Anything after that? Well, that's just icing on the cake.

So I wait, my large body braced against the counter. The very one I watch the little shit back my girl into.

Okay, so maybe I didn't have just the one target in mind tonight.

Besides, why should Michael have all the fun?

CHAPTER NINE

Charlie

My head is down when I walk back into the cabin, so I don't see him at first, but once I make it a few steps into the kitchen, I know I'm not alone.

The sound of my scream rings out at the same time my hand launches a glass bottle across the kitchen before I can even blink.

Who knew I had the reflexes of a ninja?

Reflexes, maybe. Skill? Definitely not.

As the large man easily twice the size of Dale dodges the projectile, I make a break for the doorway leading into the rest of the house.

I need to warn everyone. Plus, it will take all six of us to kick this guy's ass.

But the air barely leaves my lungs before his large hand covers half my face. He is all muscle, as his arms snake their way around me tight enough to squeeze out any chance of screaming or even talking.

I can barely breathe.

And the fight quickly leaves me. My struggles ease until I'm barely trying to escape his tight grasp.

His hot breaths sound against my ear, muffled by that creepy fucking Halloween mask.

I've seen something similar every time I force Amy to watch Batman with me, not that I had to say more than the name Christian Bale to get her to watch it.

The thought reminds me that my friends are upstairs, clueless that a masked weirdo has me restrained in the kitchen.

With what little strength I have left, I try to force my body forward and away from him. But it doesn't work. His hand is bruisingly tight on my waist, his forearm crushing my stomach.

His other hand has not moved from muffling my screams. I try to suck in air, but I can just smell him, taste him.

I'm only able to take short, shallow breaths. The lack of oxygen starts to get to me, and a nauseous, dizzy feeling rolls through me from my head to my stomach, where it settles heavy and uncomfortable.

I'm going to be sick. My throat screams in pain for air. Oh God, can you pass out mid-vomit?

Struggling isn't working. He just holds tighter, and my fight leaves with my air. I slump back, leaning into his hold.

My arm feels heavy, and my hand small against

his. The glove covering his hand is soft as I tap it with mine.

I keep my touch soft and gentle, hoping he will understand. I'll keep quiet if he lets me breathe. If he lets me live for a moment longer.

My vision is darkening, the small light in the room almost completely gone. That's when he moves.

CHAPTER TEN

Daniel

My arm rises with her stomach as Charlotte sucks in as much air as she can, but her lungs protest, and her body shudders against mine as she coughs and coughs.

"Slow, deep breaths," I encourage, stroking her throat with my hand.

I feel the whimper she gives at my voice modulator before I hear it.

We stand there quietly as Charlotte tries to control her sputtering coughs.

Her scream earlier surprised me, though it shouldn't have. She's terrified, just like the rest of them were.

But she's different. We're different. I expected her to know, somehow, that it was me.

That at that moment, she was safe from death, but perhaps she knows what is to come is so much worse.

That the life she knew has gone, and the life we will have together started this morning when she stepped out in front of my truck.

Music turns on upstairs, and I wonder if it is my brother, but I know Michael, and whichever couple he chose first, should already be dead.

Besides the first scream, there hasn't been much noise from the second floor, but that's how we work.

Quickly and quietly at first, and when there is no worry of anyone else overhearing, we can have as much fun as we want.

But the thrill of the kill is the same for me. Quiet fear or loud screams, it all gets my blood flowing.

But tonight is different. I am here for a new reason.

We changed our plans tonight; for me.

I appreciate that. Letting Michael take the lead seems the least I can do. Besides, I am not going home empty-handed. My night isn't over.

It has just begun.

CHAPTER ELEVEN

Charlie

I have barely caught my breath before registering the rest of my body.

My back hunches forward as far as I can with him unwilling to let me go. Not even for my coughing fit.

His strong arm remains latched around my belly, his hand fixed on my hip. His other hand now holds my neck, and my skin blazes everywhere. I feel his body pressed against mine, but I am most aware of the pulsing between my legs and the wetness in my panties.

And I don't know what caused it; the feel of his obviously large dick pressed into my back or the fact that despite his harsh grip on my neck, his touch is soft and gentle, almost soothing.

What I do know is that I'm fucked either way, and that at the thought of that actually happening, of this huge wall of muscle pushing me over the counter and fucking me until I can't stand, makes my pussy spasm. My inner walls pulse painfully like I need him to survive.

I shift my hips, squirming against him. I can't help it. My body reacts on its own.

What the fuck is the matter with me?!

I'm in the middle of what I can only assume is a robbery, and my body reacts in a way that it never has before . . . well, once before.

Thoughts of my actions earlier today and what I let Daniel do to me make my face heat and my body throb harder.

But that was different. Even with Michael in the car, I felt safe and protected.

But this man is a criminal. He broke in and attacked me. Well, he walked in. I did leave the door open, I suppose. And I guess he hasn't actually attacked me, just restrained me and stopped me from alerting the others.

No, Charlie!

But I don't get a chance to argue with myself for long before another masked man joins us in the kitchen . . . from the hall leading to the rest of the house.

Like the man behind me, he is dressed in all black except his mask. It's not the same as the other man's. This one is white, shaped around his face, with a large red mouth painted on. A black material flows from the edges of the mask to shield his hair.

It's sinister and creepy.

But it's not the mask alone that makes my heart stop. It's the splashes of blood that paint it. His bright and light eyes are a shade of blue that reminds me of something I can't quite put my finger on. But the saying the eyes are a window to the soul could not be truer than right this second because I can see right into the soul he doesn't have. He's excited and in his element.

What the fuck has he done?

My cry of distress is muffled once more by my capturer's hand, though this time, at least, I can breathe.

CHAPTER TWELVE

Daniel

I smother Charlotte's frantic cry, the sight of Michael sending her into near hysterics.

Her small body shudders against mine. Although muffled, I can still hear what she's trying to ask.

"Who?" She wants to know which of her friends are gone.

Michael either can't understand her or chooses to ignore her, but when Charlotte doesn't get the answer she needs, her imploring eyes turn to me.

Her body fully sinks into mine, her chin raised so high that the back of her head rests on my chest.

My whole body tingles from not just the contact but also the way she's looking at me; like I can fix this for her.

And excitement runs through me even stronger.

The need to get her beneath me is unbelievable, almost unbearable. Because despite her being terrified, her mind knows that she needs me on some level.

"Who's left?" I ask my brother, my eyes on Charlotte the whole time.

I watch through the material of my mask, my view patchy as her eyes widen with realization that our plans are much darker than she thought. The burlap makes my vision hazy, but nothing could hide the horror that settles on her face.

"Front bedroom, two doors down on the left. A couple is in there, and they're fucking, loudly," he tells me, careful not to say my name and reveal who we are. You never know if cameras are on or if something is recording nearby.

Besides, I kind of like my girl not knowing who I am just yet. It adds a thrill that I had not expected. Let her fight her body's reaction because if her earlier squirms and beaded nipples tell me anything, Charlotte is reacting to me now just as much as she did this morning.

"I was going for the little prick who tried to use her to get his dick wet," Michael says, nodding to Charlotte. His voice is deeper than normal, distorted by his own modulator. "But his room was empty. Seems he's waiting in the back bedroom on the ground floor."

Charlotte isn't the only one who stills at Michael's words.

That little fucker! He's waiting in her room, and I don't think it's for a friendly chat.

Anger fills my chest, and I know I'll be asking my brother for another favor in the near future.

Maybe I can't give up the lead for the night, after all. At least, not completely.

Charlotte whimpers, tapping on the inside of my clothed wrist. A plea.

In my anger, my hold on her has tightened again.

Somehow, I manage to pull her even closer to my body. At this point, I don't think even water could come between us.

I breathe her in. She smells like honey and cinnamon. But under that, she smells like the woods surrounding this house, the town where I have always lived and where she will now live.

She smells like home.

I need her to understand why she needs to be with me, to know that I am not only the one who can protect her but the only one who will.

"What do you think he's doing in there, little girl?" I ask with a growl, my voice even harsher than I intended as it passes through the modulator. "What do you think he'll do if I send you in there alone? Will he want to just talk? Or will he try to force himself on you? Like he did in this very spot?" I'm being harsh and mean, but I need her to know what I have saved her from, that I am not just her villain but also her savior.

"Do you think he'd push you down and force his

cock into your pussy? Hmm? Should I let him?" It's rhetorical, of course, because I'd die before I let anyone other than myself touch her body, but Charlotte answers me anyway in the form of a whimper and a quick shake of her head.

My gloves become wet as her tears roll down her cheeks and onto my hand.

It makes my chest ache. My heart tells me to comfort her, but this is what I wanted, what I need; for her to hate him. Maybe then she'll be okay with what comes next. She'll know that it is to protect her.

But most of all, I need her to know just who she belongs to.

"No," I tell her strongly, "the only cock you'll be taking tonight and every night after is mine."

Charlotte stills at my words, her breath catching in her throat.

"I'll go in there. Let's see how he likes it when someone bigger than him decides to make him the prey."

I see the moment she misconstrues my words; the chuckle from my brother confirms it for me.

Behind my mask, I grin. "Don't worry, little one. My cock only aches for you." I thrust against her a few times, hissing as pained pleasure zaps up my spine when my zipper rubs my erection.

Fuck, I am so close to coming.

I tell myself I just need to wait a little longer, but my patience is running out.

Is this how normal people feel? All of the time? How do they survive, let alone get anything done?

I have always known I was different, even from my brother. It has never bothered me, not once, but I find myself suddenly very grateful. Anger, I can process, the love for my brother and the appreciation for my family, I'll take, but the idea of this feeling, this constant throb in my pants that Charlotte causes, is something that I can't stand for long without relieving it.

The idea of feeling that for other people, for more than just one person? *Fuck that!*

No, this one woman is more than enough for me. And given time, I have no doubt that Charlotte will get used to and maybe even grow to love the fact that I am the only person for her.

For now and always.

Right now, though, it's time to exterminate a cockroach.

I press a kiss to her head, not that she feels it through my mask.

"You don't mind if I take care of that problem, do you?" I ask my brother.

"I never mind," Michael reassures me, his words sending me back to the second year of our hunts.

I had killed our parents the year before. The result of a therapy session, Helen, our adoptive mother, had insisted we see from the moment we joined the Cromwell family at ages seven and ten.

I smirk, knowing that stabbing my father through

the eye with a screwdriver was not what poor Dr. Jamieson had in mind when she suggested we try to reconnect with the two pieces of shit who tortured us for a good part of our childhood.

But it was definitely therapeutic. The relief I felt after rivaled none.

Not even a month after moving in with the Cromwells, when I realized I no longer needed to stay awake all night to stand over my little brother's bed to guard him, had I felt so free. Christopher Cromwell would not come storming into one of our bedrooms angry, drunk, and looking for someone to take it out on.

I had felt a true kind of peace deep in my soul the night they died, the very soul that I thought our father had beaten out of me.

No, that night, those first kills . . . gave me a chance to purge my anger and hatred in a way that would allow me to behave like other people—well, close enough at least—even if only for a small amount of time.

That itch, the one that rubs at my skin and burrows into my mind and whispers, telling me to lash out, to hurt something, that the man yelling at his wife would be quiet with a knife in his neck, had returned within a few months.

We found that it helps when I spend most of my year hunting, waiting, and anticipating. A necessity to keep the law at bay. Too many kills would gain attention even from our dumbass sheriff or, at worst, gain federal attention.

This year would have been the Clarkes' turn. A family, headed by Andrew Clarke, the town's mechanic and raging alcoholic. I doubt he is the only one in this town with little to do, but he is the only one I know of with a fondness to knock around his wife and stepdaughter.

The weasel quickly shot to the top of my list after I noticed the bruises on his stepdaughter's wrist while she was at my parents'. Lulu being a close friend of my sister made it easy to find out who had caused it.

The only people more loose-lipped than the town's old ladies . . . the teenage girls.

They know everything. And while it's normally a case of they only think they do, when it comes to gossip . . . they actually do.

But the Clarkes get a reprieve this year. Right now, I need to take care of my girl's problem.

CHAPTER THIRTEEN

Charlie

"Take her," the contorted voice demands behind me.

What?! No! Oh God. I'm about to die, aren't I?

The heat of his body leaves me feeling cold, and a shiver runs down my spine at the knowledge that he's abandoning me.

Something has to be seriously wrong with me. First, Daniel, and now this potentially homicidal masked burglar.

My mind flashes to Laura. Are she and Billy okay?

I cringe as I'm pulled into the other man's chest . . . his bloody chest.

I can feel the wetness, and any hope he'd rolled around in a puddle somewhere evaporated as soon as the copper scent hit my nose.

"No," I whimper out, a sob choking me.

My hands tremble as I reach up and pat at his wide body. I don't think, I can't think of anything else other than finding out how much blood has soaked into his black sweater.

His body shakes under my hands, but I just keep patting at his chest.

The wool is saturated. I don't even try to stop my cries as they leave me.

A hand twice the size of mine wraps around my wrist and rips my hand away from the sweater.

I look back over my shoulder and up at my masked man as he holds my arm away from the bloodied clothes.

My masked man? I need a fucking shrink. If I make it out of this, I might just check myself into a psych ward. Overly horny and attracted to dangerous men. Do they have pills for that?

"No." His tone is as short as his words. He's mad and not just mental mad. But furious mad.

I can't see his eyes because of the mask, but that doesn't stop my skin from feeling his gaze. It's as if he ran his hand down my whole body only to stop between my legs. The throb there matches the one in my wrist, where his strong grip still holds me.

"Easy, brother, she was just checking the blood," my masked man says slowly, like he's talking to a wound-up animal.

Brother?

"She's not thinking, just worried about her friends. She doesn't know better. I'll have to teach her not to touch other men. Not to touch you," he adds.

The pressure on my wrist doesn't move. The tension in the room stays the same until, eventually, the man in front of me breathes deeply. "I know. And you know I wouldn't touch her like that. She's yours. That makes her my sister."

The two brothers nod at each other as if they have come to an understanding.

My mind spins, and I feel foggy as my brain tries to process his words. Something nudges at the back of my mind, trying to poke its way in.

But I ignore it. Whatever it is, it doesn't matter. What matters is this: me, my friends, and making it out alive. Those of us who are still alive, at least.

"Laura," I cry. Raising my free hand, I bring it back down quickly and as hard as I can, hitting the man in front of me with the heel of my hand.

The prick is a solid wall, but he does flinch as my hand strikes his chest.

"Go," he tells his brother. Even with the altered tone, I can hear the strain in his voice. "I'm okay."

Oh, well, as long as he's okay!

My captured wrist is suddenly free from the man behind me. The blood rushing back gives me a pins-and-needles sensation. It flops uselessly onto the large man before me. The wet sweater makes a sound that has me gagging.

A large hand settles onto the crown of my head

before running over the back to my neck over and over until my stomach stops churning.

It's an effort to soothe me, but it's in vain. Two strange weirdos crept into the house, possibly killed two of my friends, and planned to do God knows what to the rest of us. And somehow, the big scary, creepy, hot wall of muscle wearing a mask made of burlap thinks that stroking my hair will make this okay.

Ugly sobs rip their way out of me from deep within my chest.

This was supposed to be a relaxing girls' weekend. How had it gone so badly?

The hand on my head freezes like he's unsure of what to do or how to make this better. *Like he fucking could!*

The music pulses around us, and the beating in my head soon matches it in rhythm. Had it always been this loud?

My breaths get short. I'm struggling to get enough air. Can you have a heart attack at twenty?

"Ssshhhh," a computer-altered voice tries to soothe now from beside me. His heat is back, and his other hand settles on my body, too—this time on my stomach. He rubs gently but firmly back and forth, and the hand on my head lowers to my back. Its actions mirror that of his other.

It's not working. My mind reels with images of what might have happened upstairs. Of what could happen down here.

I am not in control of myself anymore.

A loud smack echoes through the kitchen as if the music upstairs isn't even playing. It takes far too long for both my brain and my body to register what it was, which is probably why he does it again and then again.

The sound slaps out at the room over and over until the heat in my ass finally registers.

This motherfucker just spanked me. Hard!

My senses come to me just in time to twist my hips in an attempt to miss the next swing. I am semi-successful as it lands on my hip.

"Hmm." That's the only sound my assaulter makes as if he's pissed he missed his target.

The gloved hands of the man before me wipe at my face, clearing off my tears, but more soon replace them as the coppery smell fills my nose once more, only this time stronger. And somehow, I just know. Tears are no longer the only reason my cheeks are wet.

Happy that I have settled enough, the heat beside me pulls away, and slowly, his hands on my ass and tummy leave me, too.

"I've got her." The words come from the one in front of me, but I ignore him. Instead, I look next to me where the other one is and plead with my eyes for him to stay.

I don't know him, and he fucking terrifies me, but I do know that out of the two of them, I'm safer with him.

When that has no effect, I turn to begging. I'm not above it. There is a time to be prideful and a time to survive.

"Please, please don't leave me. I wanna stay with you," I stammer out.

My words visibly affect him. I watch as he stands taller, his chest somehow becoming broader. But he doesn't try to touch me or bring me closer to him.

My lip trembles, and my body shakes. I refuse to consider why his lack of comfort upsets me.

The two brothers face one another, towering over me. Although only one set of eyes is in view, it's like they share a look, a silent conversation between the two of them.

Their height allows them a moment of privacy, like I'm not even here.

The one before me in the white mask blinks, and his eyes soften in the dim light when they shift to me and back.

He gives his brother a sharp nod, and the skin around his eye's shifts. He's smiling.

Both of their attentions turn to me. I may only see one set of eyes, but I can feel two. Whatever they just communicated was about me, and somehow, that made me feel better.

"Be a good girl." Those parting words are whispered, as much as they can be with the altered voice, right before he kisses my forehead. His mask scratches at my skin, then he turns and leaves.

My heart drops when he turns the corner, and I lose sight of him.

Arms wrap around me tightly, wedging my arms between us, but that doesn't stop me from kicking out. This only earns me a light laugh. One that tells me he thinks my attempt at freedom is cute.

But when I manage to connect the top of my shoe with his shin, he stops chuckling.

Oh shit.

His eyes widen, mirroring my own. When I pull my foot back and do it again, harder, I don't know which of us is more shocked.

But I know who is madder.

He doesn't need words to tell me; his eyes tell me just how furious he is.

A whimper slips out of me, but his eyes don't soften like I imagine the other ones would have.

Instead, he lifts me off the ground and carries me out of the house. Amy and Jason's music easily drown out my cries of outrage and fear. By the lack of response from the man carrying me, I'm not sure he even hears me.

He doesn't stop until we're outside the downstairs bedroom at the back of the house. The one I will be sleeping in or was sleeping in, I guess.

I can't let myself think like that. That is a road to go down later because the only place it leads to is my breakdown.

My feet touch the ground slowly, my captor careful, his hands gentle as he lowers me.

Soft and steady hands hold my shoulders when I sway slightly. Once he's sure I'm not going to faint on him, he tucks a finger under my chin, forcing me to look at his face.

The white mask stands out so much among the blackness of his clothes and the darkness surrounding us that it startles me, almost like I had forgotten he was wearing it.

That same finger moves to just in front of my face as he says, "No!" The red-painted lips on the mask may be smiling, but it's clear by his tone that he's not. Not even an altered voice can hide his annoyance.

I don't know what to do. I can barely breathe right now, never mind give him a verbal response. If I could make a sound, I would be screaming.

But he's clearly not happy with my lack of reaction.

The hand on my shoulder turns my whole body to the side, and I watch as his arm rears back and then shoots forward, landing a solid spank to my ass.

The already sore skin blazes under my jeans.

His strike is lighter than the other man's, not that I'm about to tell him that.

"No kicking. You behave for me as you would for him," he tells me, pointing back toward the kitchen where we just left.

I nod, my head moving without my permission. Not one part of me wants to make the other one mad or disappoint him. Those same parts of me don't want to think or know what that says about me, either.

With our new understanding that I will not misbehave in place, he turns us to face the house.

Although the curtains are open and the room dark, it's easy to make out a figure walking back and forth inside the room.

Dale.

He doesn't see us; he's not even paying attention. His arms flail around like he's arguing with himself.

Dale is so caught up in whatever he's doing that he doesn't see the door open or the large masked man who slips inside the room.

No!

Dale may be an absolute asshole who needs more than a talk with the local sheriff, but he doesn't deserve to die.

Would he have killed you? What would he do with you once he was done, little one? a voice whispers in the back of my mind. It's taunting and cruel, but that's not what scares me. What scares me is the voice that sounds like me, but it can't be because she's agreeing with him.

Maybe Dale does deserve what's about to happen.

But Laura and Billy didn't.

It is that thought, those names that pushes my body forward. I rush to the window, hoping to warn Dale of his danger.

But I'm not quick enough. Strong arms wrap around me, restraining me before I can make it more than three feet closer to the house.

I drag air in through my mouth, but a gloved hand muffles my scream. I have no choice but to watch helplessly.

"Hush. No screaming, remember? I don't think you want me to have to tell my brother you weren't a good girl now, do you?"

No. My mind answers him instinctively.

Blunt nails dig into my cheeks a little as the hand covering my mouth squeezes when I fail to answer.

I barely shift my head back and forth, but it's enough for him to feel it.

Together, we stand in the darkness outside the lodge. Our energies mix and flow around us in the cold winter air. Fear and excitement are so strong it's hard to tell where one ends and the other begins.

The large figure's clothes allow him to blend into the darkness along the edge of the room, but not even the shadows can hide something that big completely.

What stands out the most to me is the glint off the massive kitchen knife secured in his right hand.

When the hell did he grab that?

The first strike is to the gut, low and to the left. Dale had barely finished turning before the knife was plunged in.

The big guy spins Dale with a hand on his shoulder. He wants Dale to look at him, to see him, to know the attack is coming.

The next comes just as quickly as the one before. The big guy steps back, his feet barely touching the ground, before jumping into another attack. He moves back and forth as if the two are dancing, except Dale is an unwilling partner.

He stumbles around the room, trying to dodge the slashes that strike his face and arms.

The attack lasts forever yet is over within minutes. It's relentless and playful at the same time.

I may not be able to see his covered face, but I don't need to, to know that he's smiling. This man is in his element.

He's the embodiment of confidence, excitement, and enjoyment.

I look up at the higher windows, hoping to see some kind of movement, although I'm not sure why there would be. Amy and Jason are in the front of the house, and even if they weren't, the music is more than loud enough to cover the sounds coming from downstairs.

No one is coming to help, and from the defeated way Dale stumbles toward the bedroom door in an effort to escape, he knows it, too. Hands seize his shoulders and push him, helping him toward the door.

I watch in confusion. Why would he let Dale escape?

He's not.

Any hope I feel sizzles quickly, and my stomach drops. One quick, swift kick to the back of his knees and Dale is face down on the bedroom floor.

I cry out into the hand covering my mouth and try

to pull away. A tap on my hip warns me. A reminder of what will happen if I don't settle down.

Dale is dragged the rest of the way to the door by his short hair, where he is unceremoniously dumped.

The door is pulled wider.

The large man stands over Dale, looking down at him. His broad chest expands deeply as he catches his breath.

Like he's savoring the moment. Making it last.

I can't tear my eyes away and dare not even blink.

His head turns toward us. He knows we're out here, that I'm out here. Our gazes lock. Through the mask, I can feel it. My whole body has lit up. A fire runs through my veins, and a pulse settles low, deep in my belly. The beats match my heart.

Our connection holds me hostage. He straightens his back, and somehow in that second, he becomes even bigger, wider.

The door swings closed . . . with Dale's head in the doorjamb.

My whole body flinches.

I don't look down at Dale. I keep my eyes on my guy. It's the only thing I can do right now as I swallow down bile. I flinch as the door opens and closes a second time.

And again.

And again.

It feels like I'm in the room with them. I can hear the sound of Dale's skull crunching as it's being bashed against wood, over and over.

He finally releases me from his invisible hold when he turns away and steps over Dale's prone form.

Sobs wrack my body. I don't even know how I get into the kitchen or into the arms of a killer. But here I am, surrounded by the smell of iron once more.

I feel his chest rumble as he tries to make shushing sounds to soothe me and strokes my back.

It's not working.

I don't know how long we stand here, but it's long enough for a third hand to join the soothing as it firmly squeezes the nape of my neck.

"We are running out of time, brother." The warning is gentle, like he hates that he has to interrupt us.

There's no audible reply from the man holding me, but he must have signaled somehow because his brother pushes on.

"I'll go up and take care of the other two." My blood turns to ice at his words. "Leave out the back as planned."

I'm not going anywhere, not without warning my friends!

The scream that leaves me is short-lived. His gloved hand cuts me off. The speed of it forces an oomph sound past my lips. The hand at the back of my head holds me just as tightly, the two working in sync to shut me up. The tightness of his fingers on my face tells me how furious he is.

I look at his brother beside us, whose eyes tell me how disappointed he is in my actions.

The room has frozen, and my heart beats in time to the music floating from upstairs. After a few minutes, when no other movements sound, the man beside me in the white mask gives us a nod.

He's going upstairs.

I cry more even though I know it won't do anything to save Amy and Jason. I hit the chest I'm pressed against even though it won't stop the horror about to happen.

The left hand holding the back of my head drops, the smacking sound telling the man in front of me where it went. White mask just spanked me, this time while his brother is here. And even though it's not the worst thing to happen tonight or even remotely the most shocking, embarrassment fills me. My face heats, and I drop my eyes, avoiding looking at either of them. Why does it feel different when his brother spanks me?

"Clearly, a good spank isn't enough for her. Maybe she's a more visual learner," the white mask suggests.

The words hang in the air between the three of us. What does he mean?

I get my answer when I suddenly find myself being pulled up the stairs behind them. I dig my feet into the old linoleum floor, my tennis shoes scuffing as we go. I don't stand a chance, not as he drags me and certainly not when he lifts me.

"No, no, no," I chant as we make our way up.

I watch his brother round the banister at the top of the stairs.

"Please, please. I don't want to see this." He's not listening.

Twisting the top of my body, I reach out to get a grip on the wall. Old wallpaper embeds under my nails, but my actions don't slow him down, not one bit.

His burlap mask stares at me blankly. His hands pull at my waist, maneuvering me where he wants as if I am a doll that weighs nothing at all. He turns me, and together, we stand on the last step, my back to his front with my feet dangling. Our bodies press together tightly, but his left hand sits on my stomach, pulling me in even closer, enough that I can feel the ridges of his stomach muscles as they ripple, and the thickness of his cock presses against the seam of my ass.

His right hand reaches up and grasps under my chin, lifting my head.

The bedroom door is open. We are to the left of the room, but I can see inside clearly enough.

I'm trapped, forced to watch as the masked man walks toward the bed.

Amy and Jason are lost in each other, oblivious to their surroundings.

I want to shout out, to warn them, but I can't. Something inside is telling me not to. It's like I am shut inside of my own body, a spectator to a horror show.

And so, I stand watching as Amy throws her head

back. Her naked body bounces as she rides Jason, her long red hair tumbling down her freckled back.

The smell of sex wafts out of the room, mixed with their moaning. All three of us stand there and watch as the two bodies on the bed move together, the sight both erotic and terrifying.

I squeeze my eyes closed; I don't want to watch this!

The hand on my throat tightens in a warning. The owner of the grip silently tells me to open my eyes and to keep them that way.

I do, too scared to do anything but obey.

Jason's words are drowned out by the music, but he pushes Amy to move quicker, pleasure written all over his face as he thrusts into her. He's close, lost without thought or awareness.

But maybe it's best this way. He's lucky. His eyes are screwed shut, so he doesn't see as the large man walks toward them, doesn't stop thrusting, and his grip on Amy's hips doesn't loosen until it's too late.

Her hair is fisted, and her body is pulled backward until it bows.

I scream at the same time she does. Only hers turns into a horrific gurgle as a knife is plunged into her chest, right between her breasts.

I slump forward. The hand restricting my airway momentarily cuts off my supply, and a thrill runs through me.

I just watched my friend die and did nothing to save her. Maybe dying like this is what I deserve.

But when my captor starts to carry me down the stairs by my waist, I know it won't be that easy for me. It isn't going to be that quick.

His heavy breaths push through the fabric of his mask and hit the back of my neck.

Self-loathing and disgust roll through me at the same time as a pulse settles between my legs, not that it ever truly went away.

My nipples pebble, the hardened nubs brush his forearm, and I know with every fiber of my being that he felt it.

He walks us through the kitchen—the same one where he and his murdering brother had tried to comfort me just minutes before—and out past the back of the house where I had stood and watched him beat a man to death.

This man is an animal, a killer, and my panties have never been so wet as he carries me over to an awaiting truck.

Even hidden in the shadows, how did I not see this earlier? Too caught up in my rage, I had been oblivious to my surroundings.

Something tingles at the back of my mind, the same thing that had bothered me earlier when this night had first gone to shit with the arrival of the brothers.

It went to shit the minute Dale tried to drug and force himself onto you, my inner voice reminds me. Not that it's helping right now.

It gets darker as we move farther away from the

house, the truck hidden at the edge of the tree line. Blackness consumes everything around us, and shadows swallow everything out here, including us.

I feel the darkness creeping into my soul every second we stand here longer, eating away at me and making it as black and dark as the man towering above me.

CHAPTER FOURTEEN

Daniel

I cannot wait any longer. My patience is shot, and I can't take any more of this constant arousal.

It's pain and pleasure mixed into one. The more I think about getting between her thighs, the more excited I get, only to realize I'll have to wait. The thrill that runs through me settles in my balls, making them feel full and heavy.

I know nothing will relieve that except emptying myself inside her. The thought of what I give her taking root and her growing round with my child makes my cock twitch in my pants.

No, I can't wait.

We don't have time to fuck. I delayed us enough already, but I've killed enough people mid-coitus to know there's more than one way to scratch this itch.

Charlotte has simmered down and no longer fights me, making keeping her in my arms much easier as I open the driver's side door, my truck loudly protesting as the metal squeaks.

The sound is too loud in the stillness of the cold night air. It brings the woman in my arms out of her thoughts, and suddenly, my good girl is gone.

Her squirms force me to bend and drop her onto the cab seat. No sooner does her cute ass touch down than she tries to flee past me.

Running will not be tolerated, and that's a lesson my girl will learn right fucking now.

A growl rips out of my throat as her little body shoots past me. My girl is quick, but I'm faster. My arm launches out over her shoulder, and I latch my hand onto her throat.

The noise that escapes her is like nothing I've heard her make before. A cross between a gasp and a choke.

I want to hear it again, only this time as she swallows my cock.

But first, a swift lesson.

Pulling Charlotte in close, I inhale the smell of her, her messy hair tickles my face where most of it has escaped her hair tie.

Together, we stand there, our chests heaving. The cold night burns at my lungs.

"You will not do that again," I warn her.

She doesn't respond, but I don't need her to.

I shuffle forward, using the sheer size and strength

of my own body to guide her back to the opening between the truck door and the cab bench.

"I'm going to lift you. Once in the truck, you will lie on your side, your ass touching the back of the seat, legs bent. Your knees will point toward the steering wheel," I order. "Do you understand?"

Charlotte nods, but with a tightening of my hand, I wordlessly demand her to speak.

"Yes."

When the pressure remains, my good girl adds, "Sir . . . Yes, sir."

Perfect.

I release her but regret it instantly as her body leaves mine. Charlotte has placed both hands onto the seat and starts to lift herself in.

The little hop she does before placing a knee onto the bench makes me chuckle. I guess we can't all be six feet seven.

The glare she sends me over her shoulder lets me know she is not impressed and also earns her raised ass a nice slap.

I watch and wait as she crawls farther in, turns and lays down on her side, her knees bent and facing the front of the truck . . . just like I told her.

"Good girl," I praise her.

A shiver runs through her at my words.

I need her closer, and the ruffling of the tree leaves around us is a reminder that I need to hurry.

I would say the quicker we handle the punishment, the quicker we get to enjoy what will come after, but I'm pretty sure I'm about to enjoy this just as much.

Quickly, before Charlotte can realize what's happening, I grab her at the ankles. Giving her a sharp tug, I don't let up until her ass is near the edge of the seat, close enough that her thighs still rest on the soft fabric beneath her hips while her legs hang out of the truck.

"Stay," I growl. My throat hurts, but I need her to know what I expect.

One day, she'll be able to tell what I want with just a look, the same as I will know what she needs from me by her body's movements.

We both moan as my right hand slides up her calf to the back of her knee. The tight denim does nothing to hide the curve of her muscles and the feminine feel of her body.

She fights me as I try to open her legs, forcing me to pry them apart. My large hands engulf her knees as I hold them both flat; one to the seat of the bench, the other to the back of the seat, her legs forming a perfect V. One that holds my prize between them.

Charlotte looks at me from down the length of her body, her eyes heavy, hooded with arousal.

I watch as she takes in the large bulge at the front of my pants, and her lip disappearing between her teeth is the last straw.

My control snaps.

I step forward between her feet, sliding my hand close to that hidden prize I want so badly to claim.

Will I be the first? The only one?

I want to ask, but now is not the time. Besides, it's something I'll find out tonight whether my girl tells me or not.

Finally, our bodies get to touch in a way I have wanted since we met at the gas station, and the regret I have for not fucking her against the bathroom door vanishes. This is where we were meant to be, for Charlotte to be able to see my true self and desire me anyway.

I rub my hips between her thighs.

The pleasure it causes is unexpected. My back arches, and I thrust into her. A gasp rips out of her. Her small hand grips my forearm, and she pushes her ass toward me, grinding down onto me.

Fuck! Fuck! Fuck!

I squeeze my eyes closed and draw in a deep breath. It takes everything in me to step away, but I do.

"Stay!" One last squeeze of her inner thighs and I move my hands to my belt.

Our eyes meet as the metal clinks together.

Her throat bobs when she swallows, but the light lift of her hips tells me fear is not the only thing she feels, and my good girl won't fight me anymore.

The feeling of leather pulling through the hoops on my pants has never felt so good.

Charlotte lays there watching, her eyes never leaving my hands.

I double the leather over, placing the ends together.

Once I'm ready, I give two gentle taps to her left inner thigh. I want her to know what's coming, so she can anticipate but also so she doesn't startle.

Moving would only harm her and not in the way I intend to.

I shift my right foot behind me to brace myself for the swings. Tearing my eyes away from my intended target, I watch her chest rise rapidly, her excitement just as high as mine.

When I'm sure she won't move, I draw my belt back before swinging forward and expertly striking my target.

"Ahhh," Charlotte screams, the sound echoing out for no one but my brother to hear. Her upper body rises off the bench.

We stare at each other. It doesn't matter that she can't see my eyes.

For a second, everything around us freezes, and the air in my lungs stays there. Is this where my perfect night ends? Will my perfect girl choose fight and flight?

But she is just that, my perfect girl. Slowly, Charlotte lies back down, tentatively as if not to anger me.

I smile behind my burlap mask, and warm air hits my face as I laugh. I'm not angry. I'm fucking thrilled.

"Good girl." I nod.

The next strike earns me a scream just as loud as the first, though her upper body stays on the bench this time. The one after that is followed by a moan and then another.

On and on until my Charlotte lays inside my truck shattered and needy. Equally pain-filled and horny.

Exactly how I want her.

The seam of her jeans is wet enough that the denim has darkened, and I wonder if one of her screams was from an orgasm.

God, I hope so.

I walk closer, closing the distance between us, and throw my belt on to the dashboard.

I want to lean down and fuse my lips to the wet seam of her pants. To lick and suck at her arousal before making my way up her body and show her what we taste like together. But I'm not ready for her to see my face, for that thrill of our game to be up.

Besides, no matter how much I want to feel the softness of her lips on mine, I want to feel them somewhere else even more. I grin, trying to catch my breath, and encourage Charlotte to shuffle over enough for me to slide onto the seat behind the wheel.

She sits with her back against the other door. Her legs remain parted, spread wide to stop them from touching. It makes me smile wider, and a deep chuckle escapes me before I can stop it.

"You did good," I praise, not wanting her to take my humor the wrong way.

The sound of a sniffle fills the cab. The whimper of pain that follows wraps around me, trapped inside with us now that the door is tightly closed.

She doesn't speak, and neither do I.

The sound of my zipper is loud. I watch in what little light there is as Charlotte's eyes widen, her gaze glued to my crotch, where my hand disappears into my pants.

I widen my legs and scoot forward, getting comfortable as my hand wraps around my furious cock.

It's hot and heavy in my palm.

I give it a tight squeeze and hiss as I pull it out of my pants. My chest heaves, and even though I know I won't last long once the warmth of her mouth wraps around me, I give the large head a few tugs, enjoying the pain-filled arousal that zaps down my back.

"Come here, Charlotte." I pant. She doesn't ask how I know her name. She doesn't speak at all.

When I hear no movement, my head snaps in her direction. A growl is her only warning that I will not be telling her twice.

I hear her swallow hard, the bob of her throat hidden by the shadows.

My hand rotates, keeping my pleasure on the edge as I watch her body pitch forward. She slowly crawls across the truck seat. The distance between us suddenly feels like yards rather than inches as I wait for her to reach me.

But now she kneels next to me, height on her side for once as she looks down at me, and I have no idea what to do with her.

Her chest heaves just as mine does. My gaze

lowers to where her breasts rise and fall. The wool of her sweater somehow accentuates their curves.

I have watched more people than I would have liked fucking. When hunting my prey, I like that it's their most vulnerable time, locked in passion and ignorant of everything around them. It keeps them oblivious to me until I'm ready to be seen.

I want to be rough. I want to watch Charlotte choke on my cock and listen to her swallow me.

Instinct has gotten me to where I am in life so far, so why argue with it now?

Fuck, I want this. I need her.

For the first time on a kill night, my one free day of the year, I stop thinking and let my body take over.

My right hand lands on her stomach, spanning almost the entire width. The sweater is soft under my skin, softer than I remember, and it makes me wonder what her skin beneath it feels like.

My hand roams up her body, stilling, resting between her twin mounds. I can feel the curve of them under my palm and have to fight myself to focus.

We won't be here for much longer. I have limited time.

Later, I tell myself.

Charlotte gasps as my hand curls around the front of her neck, my grip strong. The noise fuels my arousal past a point that I thought was even possible, and something in me snaps.

It's not the darkness that I'm used to, and it's not

the part of me that decides if someone lives or dies. No, this is something else entirely.

I pull her toward me slowly until her lips brush mine over the mask. Charlotte's hands fall forward, planting on my thigh to brace her.

As if I would let her fall.

"Behave," I warn, the deepness of the voice modulator adding an extra layer to the unspoken threat.

This time, I feel as she swallows, and the sensation causes images of her swallowing my essence to flood my mind.

My nose nudges hers as I move my hand to the back of her neck.

Charlotte doesn't fight me. Her body folds over until her head is in my lap, inches above where I need her.

Nothing happens for a brief second, so I shake her neck slightly.

Just as I am thinking of what to say, I feel it.

Wet and warm, she swipes her tongue out to lick the liquid beads off my cock. The sensation is like nothing I have ever felt before.

Charlotte does it again and again.

I stare at the back of her head as her tongue roams over me. It trails down my length and over my fingers that still hold it.

Her hot breath hits my fingertips at the same time as her tongue. And then she sucks one, drawing a digit into her mouth.

I jump in my seat, startled.

What the fuck was that?

In my shock, I released my cock. It sways before the weight causes it to drop and hit my stomach with a loud smack.

Charlotte chuckles, and the vibrations of it run up my arm.

A quick slap to her ass brings her back to focus.

Her hand wraps around me first, her fingers not able to touch, and then her lips are on me, swallowing me down.

Fuck!

A groan rips out of me, my head falling back when I can no longer hold it up. It's everything I thought it would be and more.

If it feels this good to be in her mouth, what will it be like to be buried inside her pussy?

I need her to suck harder, to go deeper. These desires make me fist her hair and push her down.

Gagging noises only spur me on. Turn me on more.

I bring her up for air for a second, and then she's choking again.

The feel of her tight throat swallowing me down is fucking heaven.

We keep doing this over and over. My hips lift as she goes down until she can't take anymore.

My hand leaves her head, but her movements don't stop. She needs this as much as I do.

I flex my fingers at the base of her back. My touch

makes her shiver. The band of her jeans is too tight for me to sneak inside, so I dip my hand below her to pop the button open. It does the trick, and my hand slides into the back easily.

Charlotte lifts her hips, kneeling on the bench now. I don't like it. She's not in control, I am.

My hand slides farther in, but as I get over the curve of her cheek, the jeans restrict me once more. My hand is too large. I can't reach her pussy, and if I go in from the front, I can't have her positioned the way I want.

So I go for the only hole I can.

Her protest is muffled when my fingers delve into the crack of her ass. Her yelp fuels me when I shove my middle finger into her asshole.

She wiggles her hips, desperate to dislodge me. But nothing could force me to move at this moment. My thick finger is buried deep in her forbidden hole as my left hand controls her head, and the suction of her mouth on my big cock is un-fucking-believable.

Her tongue teases me when I pull her off, which earns her a punishment, and I fuck her throat harder.

Vibrations of her moans mix with her gags.

Fuck, she's good at this. Too good.

And the realization makes me . . . fucking livid.

It's a good thing she can't see my face because I know it's filled with murder.

I thrust up harder and quicker into her mouth. My right ring finger joins my middle finger when I angrily wedge it into her ass.

Her hips lift, and a muffled, "Ahhh," rings out into the cab.

I use the grip on her ass to push her back down, her stomach pushing into her thighs.

I hold her head steady as I fuck her face and her ass, her body having no choice but to take what I'm giving.

The ring of her ass tightens, the pulsing telling me my woman is about to come. Just as her body gives its tightest squeeze and her muscles begin to shake, I pull out of her ass and shove my cock as far into her mouth as I can, holding her there.

So focused on what I'm doing, the knock on the window next to my head startles me, and I jump in my seat.

Michael stands outside with a wide grin spread across his face.

He's finished. It's time to go.

Reaching over, I wind the window down.

His eyes zero in on Charlotte, where she now thrashes in my lap, her fists pounding at my leg.

"You okay to drive back?" he asks.

I nod, too breathless and too wound up to talk.

"Thought for sure I'd find you out here fucking her. Decided to wait, huh?"

I don't know how he expects me to be able to answer him with my cock lodged in my girl's throat because I can't, so I nod again.

My brother chuckles and slaps me on my shoulder.

"Just make sure you drive along the tracks you made coming in, okay? Just like we discussed."

I give him a final nod just as Charlotte swallows. The muscles in her throat ripple along my thick shaft, and a groan rips out of me, my head hitting the back of the seat again.

Fuck, I'm going to come.

I lift her off long enough to start the truck and shift it into drive.

I feel everything at once. The cool night air coming in from the window touching my wet cock, the cotton of my pants where it has fallen heavy with arousal waiting for attention, and the heat of Charlotte's breath as she pants.

My hand forces her head back down the second my foot touches the gas.

Her fingers touch me briefly before she swallows me whole.

And then I'm shouting into the night. A voice that would make grown men piss themselves when they hear it is now screaming out as I pump jet after jet of cum down Charlotte's throat.

The truck keeps going, my foot pushing the gas pedal to the floor.

Pleasure races through me as the truck speeds out of the campgrounds and back onto the mostly unused dirt road that leads to my family's cabin.

I'm still coming minutes later, and it's the longest and most powerful orgasm I've ever had. Yet somehow, I know it'll be even better when I release inside her pussy, filling her with everything I have.

Once sated, I release her.

My cock leaves her with a wet pop. Strings of cum and saliva connect us as she backs away.

Charlotte glares at me, but it's offset by the red puffiness of her lips, wet with my cum. They look well-used, and the sight makes my dick twitch and harden again already.

She harshly wipes at her mouth with the back of her hand. Angrily, she fastens her pants. At first, I think it's because I had been too rough, but I watch as she presses her ass into the bench.

"Bad girls don't come," I hiss.

Her eyes drop to where my erection bobs, half hard and growing.

"You're good." I tell her, "Your mouth's been fucked before." It's not a question, and the anger in my voice is clear.

She opens her mouth, and I tip my head, silently daring her to lie to me.

Charlotte licks her lips and then gives me a small nod.

At the confirmation, I return my focus to the road, my hands tightening on the wheel.

Movement in the truck bed catches her attention. I know the moment she sees Michael and realizes we are not alone because her fuckable mouth pops open, but with the back of his head facing us, I know she doesn't recognize him.

"Once," she whispers, probably wanting our conversation to stay private.

Not that it matters. Michael is my brother, so he knows everything about me. Besides, he just saw her with my cock in her mouth.

"My only boyfriend." She sounds panicked like she needs me to understand. When I don't speak, she continues, "We barely dated! In my first year of college for like three months. Neither of us were really into it."

Her bottom lip disappears into her mouth, where she begins to chew it. "He didn't even come," she whispers even quieter.

But I hear her, and a nod is the only answer she gets.

I turn my head to her when we are a few minutes out. "Put me away," I order, lifting my hips to show her what I mean.

Her hands are hesitant as they grip me. Gently, she pulls back the top of my pants opening. Now fully hard, Charlotte has no choice but to tuck my erection into the waistband of my boxers. It instantly fights to get back out, the tight material tenting.

I hold in a chuckle as Charlotte tries to be as gentle as she can, zipping and buttoning my pants while my fat cock tries to force its way back out.

I expect her to rush away from me when she finishes, but she doesn't. Instead, she remains kneeling next to me, looking down at me.

"Don't be mad," she begs, her words hitting my

mask, and then her lips press slowly and softly onto mine. Her hands are on my thigh again to brace herself more until she squeezes my cock.

She gives it a few strokes, causing me to hiss.

Keeping my head straight, I navigate the truck toward the house now in view. My vision is filled with her as she pulls away, moving to sit back in her seat pressed against the passenger door.

I knew it at the gas station, I knew it in the house, and I knew it as she swallowed my cock—Charlotte will fight me because she thinks she should, but she wants this. She wants me.

The house gets closer, and the road illuminates with lights that reach out and touch the truck interior.

It's time.

Reaching up, I grab my mask and pull. The material passes over my head with ease.

It takes less than a second for her to recognize me, and I'm not even fully unmasked yet.

"Daniel."

The way she says my name is a cross between relief and horror, but it's mixed with a moan, and I know that out of the two, relief wins.

She's happy it's me.

I slow the truck, pulling it to a complete stop just shy of the main house where the rest of our family sleeps peacefully.

Charlotte wants me, and it's time I give it to her.

CHAPTER FIFTEEN

Charlie

I stare in confused horror, my heart pounding the same rhythm that beats just as strongly between my legs.

I'm a traitor and a whore. His whore.

I'm wet, uncomfortable, and so fucking confused.

Daniel. Why the fuck didn't I see it?

The pull I feel, the attraction. I mean, what are the chances of feeling this way about two people after never really feeling anything?

Fucking idiot!

I don't know what to say. Where would I even start? Yesterday, I would have willingly gone on a date with this man and could have envisioned a life with him despite not knowing anything but his name.

A little over twelve hours later, I know what his

cock tastes like and how it feels to have him bring me pleasure, all while he smells of blood. Blood that belongs to my friends.

He's sick . . . We both are. Maybe we really do belong together.

His hand grips my jaw. "I will be the only man you ever taste again." It's not a question. He's telling me.

My tears fall as he releases me.

I flinch when he opens his truck door. The loud and violent sound disturbs the woods surrounding us.

His brother jumps over the side of the truck, dismounting without much effort.

I watch as he grins at Daniel, saying something too low for me to hear. Their movements are familiar. How didn't I recognize them?

Had I just not wanted to see it?

Daniel returns, one hand braced on the door and the other on the truck roof, so tall that he needs to bend slightly to peer in at me.

He doesn't say anything, but now I know why my kidnapper isn't much of a talker. Daniel isn't a talker.

My lower lip trembles at the thought.

How has everything gone so wrong?

He reaches in, capturing my ankle with his hand, and I panic. Images of what I saw happen in the camp cabin flood me, and horrors of what I didn't see haunt me even more. What did Michael do to Laura and Billy?

No! No!

I can't let this happen. It's wrong; he's all wrong.

My foot connects with his shoulder, causing him to stagger back, and a look of bewilderment crosses his face.

He didn't expect me to fight.

Shit, now he's mad, like mad, mad, but even now, with his face twisted with rage as he comes toward me, something inside me tells me he won't kill me.

I'd say my heart, but how stupid would that be?

Daniel reaches inside the cab, but he doesn't go for me this time. He reaches for his belt on the dash.

Fuck, not again. My inner thighs still hurt, the pain now more of a constant heat. It doesn't help that my jeans have been rubbing the sensitive skin. The heat was quick to travel up each of my thighs, settling and meeting in the middle.

Every time it starts to lessen, my pants rub, and I'm reminded of what he did . . . of what I let him do. Of what I wanted him to do.

Even now, as his hand wraps around my leg much tighter than before, my mind screams how wrong this is while my body wants to do so much more.

I let out a quick, short, surprised scream as he pulls me across the bench seat and wraps the belt around my ankles, securing it with the metal buckle before I even sit up.

Daniel gives my bound feet a quick shake. Confused, I blink up at him only to find him glaring. Brow furrowed, he meets my gaze as he raises a pointed finger. "No," he reprimands. His voice is low and growly. Rough, like he's used it too much. It's different without the mask and voice modulator, but it still rolls through me, igniting every nerve.

I shiver as he pulls me out of the truck and throws me over his shoulder. Shame washes over me because I know the cold night air piercing through my sweater has nothing to do with my body's reaction.

But even with the guilt and shame I feel, I know as we head toward the building behind the house that I won't try to stop whatever is coming.

I won't be able to, and deep down, in a place that I will never share with anyone aloud, I know I don't want to.

CHAPTER SIXTEEN

Daniel

I barely spare a glance over the property to check for any threats. The sound of water gently lapping at the shore is lower than I know it should be.

For the first time since I was a small child, I'm unable to focus on more than one thing at a time and keep track of everything around me.

I'm at the mercy of my brother, the only person I have ever trusted to have my back.

The weight wiggling on my shoulder is the only thing I can think of. The way she smells, and the sound she makes as her fists hit my back, like she's putting all her effort into it. I try not to laugh, as I barely feel her attack. A quick tap to her ass soon calms her.

Walking toward the outbuilding, I catch sight of

movement from the corner of my eye. The curtain falls into place at the living room window before I can see a face.

Someone is awake. I don't need to look over again to know it was our mother. I have long since suspected that she knew who I was and what I encourage my brothers to be, too. Helen's insistence to come to the cabin for a family Halloween bonding session only confirmed my suspicion.

Michael can deal with her, at least for tonight.

My stride doesn't falter as I kick the outhouse door open, my hands too busy holding her squirming hips. Charlotte continues to fight me, even if only halfheartedly.

The one-room building is dark as we enter, but I know this room like the back of my hand. I use it every Halloween.

I smirk at the thought.

Mother had asked to come here, not knowing that this is exactly where Michael and I come to clean up after our hunts. Isolated and in the woods, where else would we go?

I head to the steel table that dominates the middle of the room.

I gently place Charlotte down on the left side of it, away from the tools hanging on hooks attached along the edge of the table.

She stopped fighting when we entered the dark room, not in fear but rather acceptance. I feel it flow through her as I set her down.

I had expected her to fight more, to panic as the door closed behind us, leaving us in the pitch black.

But I guess a part of her understands that you don't have to be afraid of the dark when the scariest thing in it loves you.

I need to see her, feel her, consume her.

Turning away from her, I pull the cord that illuminates the room, light flooding every inch of every corner.

Perfect, I grin, but it quickly falls when Charlotte stretches, reaching out for the hammer that sits farther down the table. Her fingertips manage to touch it, bringing it slightly closer as I close the distance between us once more.

I fight the urge to punish her again. After all, the door had been unlocked and the exit clear, but my girl had stayed, her ass still perched on the edge of the table, right where I left her.

Charlotte sits up, hammer in hand by the time I step between her knees. I hold my hand out for her newly acquired weapon of choice.

She glances at my hand for a second, the debate of what to do written clearly on her face. Finally, she gives a small pout, her bottom lip pushing out as she hands over the hammer.

Good girl. I throw it to the other end of the table. The loud bang causes her to startle. Her whole body lifts off the table and moves closer to the edge . . . closer to me.

Her body knows I will keep her safe.

My eyes zero in on her pouting lips. I want to feel them beneath mine, to taste her again.

Her gaze falls to my mouth, and that is all the encouragement I need as I lean down and steal my first kiss of the night.

Her lips are soft as I press our mouths together.

I pull back slightly to look at her face. Her eyes are wide, startled like she can't believe what I just did.

Leaning in, I do it again, but firmer. This time, I pull her pouty lower lip into my mouth, nipping it quickly before soothing it with my tongue.

Her gasp fills both the room and my chest.

I bury my hand in her hair, knotting my fingers in it as I continue to nip at and soothe her lip, pressing my lips to hers over and over in between.

At first, she freezes, but her eyes soon close, and her lips respond.

Her hands quickly find their way to my body, rubbing at my abs and up over my chest.

Her mouth swallows my moan when her nails bite into the skin of my neck.

She scratches at my skin, and I hiss. Her nails cut slightly as she tries to pull me in like she can't get close enough.

I rip my mouth away, gasping for air.

We're both panting, my body hunched over hers. One hand is buried at the base of her skull while the other grips the edge of the table so hard I'm surprised it hasn't crumpled.

Charlotte gasps, but this one is different. She sounds shocked, and a low whimper soon follows.

She's staring at her hands, her blood-coated hands.

My top is still wet, so saturated with that worm's blood that it hasn't completely dried yet.

The sight is both proof of how far I will go to have her and a reminder of how much she consumes me.

I need to clean us up.

Michael has yet to come in here. He is probably cleaning the truck first. Maybe it's his way of giving us some alone time, which I do not intend to waste.

Stepping away from her takes every ounce of self-control that I have left. Reaching behind my head, I grasp the top of my sweater and pull it over my head, tossing it aside to the concrete floor, where it lands with a wet splat.

Charlotte gags at the sound, her eyes unable to look away from where it lands.

Placing my finger under her chin, I force her focus back on me to distract her. I want to feel her eyes as I undress. I want her to watch, to see what she does to me.

Quickly, I loosen my laces and kick out of my boots. Her gaze moves, her eyes tracking my hands as I unbutton my pants.

There's no preamble as I shove them down, my cock springing free.

I hiss as the cold air of the room hits my sensitive

flesh. Even in the frigid air, my arousal cannot be deterred.

I kick off my pants, the small pile of clothes now growing, waiting for hers to join.

Throughout my strip tease, Charlotte has remained still, her eyes taking everything in as it is revealed. The minute I step closer, her body reacts. Her breath stutters as if she can't decide. My good girl is stuck between fight or flight.

And then she chooses.

Her feet hit the ground with little sound despite the small jump she has to take to get down from the table.

She has forgotten her feet are bound. I don't let her even try taking a step before my arm winds around her waist and hauls her back.

"Please, please, Daniel," she cries.

I don't know what she's begging for—her freedom, her friends, or more of me—but I suspect she doesn't know either.

Her hands push at my chest, and she tries to turn away.

Holding her steady proves tricky, so I pull her close, plastering her chest to mine. Her struggling instantly stops, and I'm able to slide my hands under her sweater.

She is soft and creamy beneath my palms while the yellow wool is rough against the back of my hands, now hardened with dry blood. I push until it bunches under her arms.

"Up."

Her body may want her to fight, but her mind doesn't. Charlotte was made to follow orders. Doing as she is told, she reaches her arms high toward the ceiling, and I rid her of the crusty wool.

She leans into me when the discarded clothes make another squelch, and a sob lands on my bare chest.

While stroking the back of her head, I hum to soothe her like I did back at the camp.

I pull at the back of her bra. How the fuck does this thing open?

I growl in frustration as the clasp refuses to release. After a particularly hard tug, small hands join mine. I watch as her nimble fingers simply flick the fucking thing, and it opens . . . she didn't even look.

I glare at the contraption when I throw it to join the rest of our clothes, making a mental note to burn it along with any others she may have.

I feel her laughter more than I hear it. Huffs of warm air caress my skin, making me tremble, and I know the fight has left her.

My hands slide between us, and it's Charlotte's turn to tremble as the back of my fingers graze her stomach. I gently dip them inside her pants, and feeling the top of her lace panties causes me to jump.

I fumble with the brass button for a minute before deciding that being careful clearly isn't my thing. Grasping both sides of her pants, I pull, and the button flies off quickly.

Much better. I smirk

Charlotte lifts her head from my chest. Her big doe eyes peer up at me as if I have the answers to everything. What is this? Why are we so drawn to each other? What happens next?

But all I know is that if I don't get inside her within the next few seconds, I'll need to kill someone else tonight.

Her chin rubs at my chest before settling. She blinks up at me with heavy eyes as I shove her pants down to her thighs. Breaking eye contact, I peer over her head to admire the curve of her ass. My hands curl around to grab the globes, giving them a rough squeeze.

My fingers span wide enough that my right ring finger tickles at her rose bud, and her whole body jolts.

I fold my large body and crouch, quickly releasing the belt and pulling roughly at her pant legs, tapping her inner thighs to show which leg to step out of. My fingers come away from her thighs damp.

Her hands rest on my shoulders for balance. Her bare breasts rise and fall quickly in front of my face.

I watch as emotions change her expression. She's still warring with herself and unable to let herself decide guilt-free. Charlotte needs me to decide. So, I make the decision for her.

Leaning forward, I inhale her scent, my nose buried in the patch of hair between her thighs before gently kissing her stomach.

The metal of my belt clangs, warning her what I am about to do, but I grip her leg just as she tries to step away, strapping them back together.

My wide hands caress her hips as I lift her back onto the table, this time so that her body lies across the width when I press her down.

Quietly, she complies—not that the hand I have on her chest gives her many options. Her eyes never leave mine as she settles back.

Stepping away, I leave my hand where it rests for a moment more, a silent instruction to stay. Her nod is enough for me to trust her, and I move away from the table. I quickly retrieve what I want from the back wall, desperate to touch her again.

Rounding the table, I stand near where her head rests. Slowly, I trail my hands from her shoulders down to her wrists. Grasping them as gently as I can, I raise them above her chest. The rope is soft, almost silky as I weave it between her wrists, knotting it when they are secured, not too tight but enough that she will feel it chafe should she pull.

I watch her hips wiggle, her thighs pressing tightly together to ease some of her need.

The wind picks up outside, and it's the first thing I've noticed outside of the bubble we created. I can't think of anything beyond these four walls because nothing else has ever been this important.

Taking the end of the rope, I pull Charlotte's hands higher, over her head, and tie it tightly to an empty hook on the end of the table.

Once secure, I waste no time in rounding the table. My feet eat up the distance, and her legs widen as I draw near.

But I need more.

Lifting her thighs, I pull her to the very edge of the table, the sound of straining metal keens out as the rope pulls tight. Bending her knees, I create a circle that I can duck into.

I manage to push my broad shoulders through the gap as I force her legs over my shoulders and down my back until her knees rest at my waist.

"Have you fucked before?" I need to know if someone has taken her before, or will this be a first we share together?

With a small whimper, Charlotte shakes her head.

Good, me neither.

When her cheeks flush and her eyes widen, I realize I spoke those words aloud.

I feel her knees bend more, and she settles her feet at the base of my back. Her thighs flex, trying to pull me closer.

I hiss as our hips meet.

Fuck, I need to calm down.

Smacking her ass, I give her a look that warns her to knock it off. She needed me to be in charge, so we'll go at my pace.

Taking the minute I need, I let my gaze roam over her. She's perfect.

I lean down, kissing my way up her stomach and over her chest, where I suckle.

The cold edge of the table bites at my thigh, and I realize that arousal isn't the only reason for her beaded nipples and goose bumps. The metal under her is freezing. I cover her body with mine, our gaze locked as I steal another kiss. Our tongues tease as we taste each other.

Reaching between us, I place myself at her entrance and coat my tip with her excitement.

I bite her lip. Keeping hold, I pull away until I'm forced to release it.

"Mine."

Thrusting forward, I push my body into hers, taking a first while giving her mine.

We cry out at the same time, pleasure and pain equally mixed.

The arm bracing me on the table buckles, and I drop to my elbow. My fingers weave their way into her hair, fisting the thick brown waves.

Her body resists, forcing me to pull back. I continue to thrust harder until I'm fully seated inside her.

Her hands have fisted, gripping the rope that binds them above her head.

Heat engulfs my cock, and pleasure runs up my spine.

I was wrong. This is so much better than punishing her.

I can't hold my head up, and it falls forward, dropping to her shoulder. "Ahhh." I pull out and plunge into her once more, my groan loud and long when pleasure spreads throughout my whole body.

"Fuck," I pant, my chest heaving.

I drop my weight onto Charlotte more, the table protesting loudly at my quick and hard thrusts.

She hisses, her body bowing beneath mine, and her knees pinned to my side.

I fist her hair tighter and lower my mouth to her breast, biting any skin I can reach before I soothe it. My right hand rises and teases the other.

I grunt as I join our bodies over and over. After a few more thrusts, her grunts turn to moans.

Pushing up, I loom over her to see her face scrunched tight with pleasure, her mouth opening to release another moan as I push in as deep as I can and stay there, grinding our hips together.

I repeat the movement, and her watery eyes meet mine as she cries out.

Standing fully, I look down to where we're connected. My cock and her thighs glisten with her arousal. I never want this to end. I push in and rub my hips to hers harder, causing her legs to shake. I need her to come before I fill her.

Suddenly, Charlotte keens and tries to twist away, forcing my grip on her hips to tighten. I pull her toward me as I thrust harshly.

When she doesn't stop trying to twist out of my hold, I tear my eyes from her body and follow her gaze.

Michael.

I watch my brother for a second as he moves around the room, collecting our discarded clothes and loading the washer. The smell of bleach registers, and I wonder if he has already bleached the cloths we use to clean the inside of my truck.

The thought doesn't linger for long.

Grabbing Charlotte's chin, I force her to look at me.

"Mine," I repeat. I'm the one fucking her, not my brother.

Charlotte tightens her legs around me, her feet digging into my back, and the slaps of our hips sound out loudly. I can feel her inner walls spasm every time a noise penetrates our fucking, a quick reminder that we aren't alone. She likes that we have an audience.

My grip becomes bruising, and I move a hand from her hip to her shoulder, pulling her to meet my thrusts even harder.

"Fuck, fuck, fuck," I chant as I feel my balls draw up tight.

Her grip on my cock tightens, and her body seizes before she cries out.

That and the sight of her breasts bouncing with each of my forceful thrusts pushes me over, and with a roar, I shove myself inside her one last time, collapsing forward onto her as my orgasm stretches on. My hips twitch back and forth in shallow movements as I pump my cum into her.

Fuck, how do people think of doing anything other than that? We have only just finished, and I already feel myself hardening at the thought of going again.

My hand aimlessly searches for her tied wrists.

Pulling at the rope, I try to free her. After a few unsuccessful minutes, I feel something being pushed into my hand and chuckle when I realize what it is.

I take the knife gratefully, panting into Charlotte's neck, and cut at the rope above where her wrists are knotted.

Still trying to catch my breath, I pull away from her just enough to smile down at her. Bright eyes stare back at me, her lip once more trapped between her teeth.

"You're perfect," I tell her, nudging her nose with mine.

She blinks up at me, and a few tears roll out, following the same tracks others have left, escaping into her hair.

Her inner muscles continue to pulse around me when her arms loop over my head, the rope resting on the back of my neck.

"Make sure you scrub both of yourselves in the shower. I'll be back to bleach that later." Michael's words ring out just before the door swings closed behind him.

Joined together, Charlotte and I lay there for a few more minutes before I pull us both up. Standing, I carry her wrapped around me like a koala, my cock still buried deep inside her, to the shower in the corner of the room, next to where the laundry cycles our clothes.

Seeing fresh clothes on top of the counter along

with a fresh towel, I make a mental note to thank my brother.

All thoughts of my brother and fresh laundry disappear as I step beneath the warm water and lose myself in my girl once more.

CHAPTER SEVENTEEN

Charlie

I blink, trying to push away the fog that closes in. My body leans back without my permission, and I try not to take comfort from the hand gripping the back of my neck.

The large wooden bed looks comfortable and cozy. I'm so tired my whole body aches. Muscles I didn't even know I had scream at me to crawl under the thick handmade blanket to sleep away the night's events.

After our shower, Daniel released my restraints before carefully drying every inch of my body. Deeming me perfect, he dressed me in one of his T-shirts . . . and nothing else.

I stood patiently, our gazes locked as he dried himself before pulling on sweats.

Hand in hand, I let him lead me from the outbuilding into the freezing night air. When I gasped in pain as a rock dug into my bare foot, Daniel slid his hands around the curve of my ass, lifting me easily and carrying me inside like I was the most precious thing he owned.

I didn't think to stop him. I just let him. Arms and legs around him, I buried my face in his neck. I felt loved and cherished as we went to his bedroom on the top floor of the house. Daniel never loosened his hold on me or slowed until he lowered me to where I now stand.

The energy around us has shifted. It's gentler. He's gentler. Like something inside him has settled.

He doesn't speak, but that just seems to be the way he is. His eyes soften as he pulls back the bed covers and waits patiently for me to climb in and lie down. The sheets are soft beneath my hands and knees as I crawl to where he waits.

Staring up at him, I feel my eyes grow heavy.

His lips twitch, and a brow rises when I lift my arms, asking him to tuck me in.

Daniel taps the mattress until I lower my arms and am cocooned. Arms in, noted.

I sigh softly, letting my body sink into the softness below me as he tucks me in tightly. The feeling of his lips brushing my forehead forces a final tear to leak out.

How can a man this sweet, this pure be a raging killer? And how can I still want him?

CHAPTER EIGHTEEN

Daniel

Charlotte falls asleep quickly, her petite form somehow looking even smaller under the thick quilt.

The sight of her in my bed causes my chest to flutter, and I don't fight the smile that creeps onto my face. I embrace the warmth that courses through my heart.

She's perfect. Tonight was perfect.

I gently brush a few strands of hair from her face. She looks exhausted. It'll take time, but she needs me just as I need her. I can feel it, see it.

Slowly, careful not to wake her, I lean down and kiss away the tears drying on her cheeks.

"Happy Halloween, baby," I whisper against her skin.

It physically pains me to leave her, but she needs

her rest, and I need to help Michael with any remaining cleanup. It's the least I can do. Although, if I know my brother, everything is already perfect.

The voices from the ground floor reach me when I step off the first floor, where the rest of my family sleeps.

It seems my mother didn't go to bed after all.

The living room had been empty when I carried Charlotte through the house, the lights off and doors closed on the family floor.

I thought we had been in the outhouse long enough for my mother to wander off to bed, but perhaps curiosity has tempted her back out.

"What do you mean, nothing?" My mother's usually calm voice hisses, "I just watched him carry a woman out back like a sack of potatoes!"

Or maybe it's guilt.

"Potatoes don't moan that loud." Michael talks back, and the sudden urge to punch him in the face floods me.

Prick. Charlotte better not hear him talk like that, even if he's joking.

Silently, I continue down the stairs. I want to listen when I'm the topic of conversation.

"He spoke, Ma. When Daniel first saw her, he spoke." My brother's hushed voice is filled with raw emotion, and I feel the pain he has felt over my lost words throughout the years. "Mine. That's the first word I heard my brother say in eighteen years. And the little fucker hasn't stopped talking all night," he tells her, his words ending with a chuckle.

His grin widens when he sees me coming down the stairs.

I raise my brow in challenge to his words, and his chuckle turns into a full laugh. "For you? You were a chatterbox." He grins at me. "And I'll do anything necessary to keep it that way," he swears.

His face sobers after a minute, and I step around my mother, the three of us now standing close.

Michael's eyes meet mine, his stare fierce. "You want Charlie?" he asks before giving me a sharp nod. "She's yours."

"Charlotte," I correct, my tone as sharp as my scratchy throat will allow, too unused to sounds passing through it.

Our mother's gasp fills the space between us, her tear-filled eyes glued to my face, searching for something.

Whatever it is, she finds it. I watch as my mother, the woman who saved my brother and me, who gave us a second chance in life, nods resolutely, her lips pinching to stop her chin from quivering.

After a few short breaths, she walks toward me, stopping when I tower over her. My mother's warm hands embrace either side of my face.

"You love her."

It's not a question, yet I nod to show her I do.

"Does she love you?"

I pause, not wanting to answer. To lessen the pain

in my chest, I shake my head, not wanting to say the word aloud.

"Could she learn to love you?"

My nostrils flare at her question, my senses filling with Charlotte as if she was in the room with us. The smell of her skin, the sound of her wet pussy echoing around me as my hips meet hers, and the feel of her moan escaping her throat under my hand. All of it gives me hope, but then I remember how she cried in the shower and how her eyes rounded in my truck when my mask came off.

And I give my mother another shake of my head.

Her gentle hands pat my cheek. She leans in close, forcing me to bend and meet her, our foreheads meeting in the middle.

"Then you had better love her hard enough for both of you, my sweet boy." Her voice breaks.

Her lips press gently to my forehead, and my eyes close as her words truly sink in.

She won't interfere. I get to keep both my family and Charlotte.

I watch as she climbs the stairs, her hand gripping the banister. "May God forgive me," she whispers, her words carrying down to where Michael and I stand.

CHAPTER NINETEEN

Charlie

I'm hot, too hot.

I huff, shoving at the covers that weigh me down. I kick them off as they tangle around my legs.

My muscles ache, a heaviness in them I'm not used to.

Splaying my arms in front of me, I stretch myself out. It feels great, so I quickly stretch my legs, pointing my toes to the bottom of the bed and releasing a noisy yawn.

The heavy weight on my waist tightens, and I glance down to see a strong, tan forearm thrown over my waist, his wide hand spanning my stomach.

I squeeze my eyes closed and groan.

It happened. All of it was real.

I just had the best night's sleep of my life on the same night my friends were brutally murdered.

And oh, yeah, one of the men responsible is spooning me.

I'm a horrible fucking human. I deserve to burn with him.

I grasp a large finger in my hand and try to lift it without waking its owner.

"Nuh-uh," a voice rumbles behind me, and I freeze.

The body behind me stays still. Daniel's chest continues to rise and fall steadily, so it wasn't him.

Twisting my neck as far as I can without waking my bedmate, I peer over at the chair in the far corner.

Michael.

Head resting on his hand, one leg folded over the other with his foot on his knee, he is the epitome of chill, and it looks like he's been there for a while.

The thought makes me shiver.

Suddenly, I am not so hot after all. In fact, I feel very cold and exposed. I eye the crumpled covers at the foot of the bed, but then I remember that he saw more than just my bare thighs last night. Given everything that has happened, Daniel's brother seeing me in a state of undress isn't really that big of a deal.

I want to ask what the fuck he's doing in here, but the tray of breakfast food and orange juice on the dresser next to him is answer enough.

"I thought Daniel might prefer for you to stay in here for a while," he states, his voice laden with sleep.

"Besides" — he smirks — "I had a feeling you might try something."

I stay quiet. What am I even supposed to say to that? The man literally caught me red-handed.

"I'm not normally such a voyeur," Michael tells me, "but given his . . ." He searches for the right word. "Inexperience, I thought he might sleep harder than normal."

I nod because it's true. Even with us talking, the man behind me has yet to stir.

"You leaving would hurt him, Charlie."

Michael's words make my eyes fill and my chest ache, the notion physically painful to me. And I hate myself just a little bit more.

So instead, I just nod.

But Michael's not finished. "There's nothing I wouldn't do to protect my brother, Charlie, even if it was something he didn't want." I swallow at the vague threat. "Do you understand?"

I nod again. But just like his brother, a raised brow is all he needs to get what he wants.

"Yes, I understand," I whisper. "Will you tell him I tried to leave?" I ask, needing to know if I'm in trouble with two brothers or just the one.

I ignore the part of myself that worries about Daniel's feelings rather than any punishment he may give.

"Do you want to eat? I brought eggs, bacon, French toast, and normal toast." He lists off what's on the tray, ignoring my question. "They're still warm."

Before I can answer, Michael disappears, my vision blocked by Daniel's wide shoulders.

The hand on my tummy slides around farther, a solid leg is thrown over both of mine, and I find myself quickly tucked beneath his big, sleepy body.

"Leave us," Daniel grumbles from where he's buried his face in my hair.

I breathe in deeply, taking in the comfort that being so close to him brings.

Michael's chuckle sounds farther away, and I know he's heading for the door.

"Don't forget to feed her." Those are his parting words like I'm some kind of dog rather than a semi-willing hostage.

Asshole.

The smell of bacon hits me again. *Okay, so maybe he's a sweet asshole just this once.*

I feel movement along the curve of my ass as the T-shirt is raised to my hips. All thoughts of breakfast are gone, and I find myself more than happy to remain beneath him a little longer.

My body disagrees loudly. My stomach rumbles, and the fingers between my legs quickly disappear.

"No," I complain.

His hand taps my ass as his body releases mine.

The bed groans under us when his huge body vaults over the end. His bare feet slap at the hardwood floor on his way into the adjoining bathroom.

I wet my lips as I look him over from my position on the bed. It's bright out, the morning light floods the bedroom, and I get a good look at Daniel's body. Last night, I had been distracted, too busy taking in the feel of him.

Besides, I spent most of the time I was awake here last night attached to him, literally. His back ripples, his muscles shifting as he shakes off and tucks himself back into his sweats.

My mouth waters at the memory of what he's hiding in there.

He side-eyes me as he washes his hands, grinning when he catches my eyes roaming his exposed flesh.

"Eat first, we'll fuck later."

I blink at his blunt words, and again, I'm reminded that Daniel is a man of few words.

"Daniel," I start, unsure how to broach the subject, scared he may get angry or worse. "What are we going to do? I need to go home soon."

Daniel's back straightens at my words. He's angry.

He doesn't answer me as he throws the hand towel onto the vanity. Silently, he carries the food over to the bed. He climbs in, settling in front of me.

"People will notice I'm missing. That my friends are gone."

He still doesn't speak as he scoops up a forkful of eggs and raises it to my mouth. A silent order. One that I happily follow.

"We eat," he tells me, "then I'll get us coffee." He continues, his eyes focused on where a piece of bacon just disappeared into my mouth. He leans forward and fuses our lips, his tongue sneaking in and stealing the food he just fed me. "And then I will fuck you again," he finishes.

Neither of us speaks after that, content to sit in silence while he takes turns feeding us. I give him a small, grateful smile as he lets me eat the last piece of bacon and the last of the syrup-dipped French toast, too.

Once every last bit of food is gone, his sticky fingers graze my mouth. My tongue peeks out to lick him, but a small taste isn't enough. One by one, I draw his digits into my mouth, swirling my tongue around his fingers and sucking before I move on to clean off the next.

His heated gaze meets mine when he raises his freshly cleaned fingers into his own mouth. "I'll go get us some coffee."

Leaning down, Daniel presses his mouth to mine, once, twice, and then a third time before he pulls himself away and whispers against my lips, "Do not touch that door handle." The sternness makes my thighs clench, and he watches my body react to him. "Good girl," he growls.

The praise only makes my body even more needy, and I am wide-eyed and panting by the time the door closes behind him.

CHAPTER TWENTY

Daniel

Charlotte's words echo in my mind as I head for the kitchen. She's right. People will notice, and someone will come looking.

We have a few days at best. But she's wrong about one thing—she's never leaving. Not now, not ever.

That woman is mine.

I don't know what startles the people gathered in the kitchen more—the grin on my face or the fact that it's eleven in the morning and I am only now rousing.

"Look who finally decided to join us!" my sister teases.

"Looks like someone celebrated Halloween too hard." Kaleb pokes me, the little shit. I kick out at his foot just as I pass.

"The pair of you, leave your brother alone," my

father reprimands. "Besides" — he grins — "I hear he brought a woman home."

I feel my face heat at his wink.

Michael, the fucking loudmouth.

"You heard or you *heard*?" Kaleb laughs, my steps faltering at his question. Michael hearing or seeing Charlotte and me is entirely different than other family members.

"Your mother told me," Dad confesses. "That all you kids got? I thought for sure you'd rib him more than that." He laughs.

I look at my mother, who has busied herself at the counter throughout this exchange, scrubbing at the same spot while clearly listening.

I need her to know what it means to me, what her loyalty means.

I stop once I am right behind her, but she doesn't turn or look at me.

Bending, I place a quick kiss on her cheek. "Good morning, Mom."

All the noise in the room evaporates. Even the hum of the coffee machine seems to dim.

All at once, my family's voices ring out together.

"Oh my God."

"What the fuck?"

"Helen, you weren't joking."

"Good morning, baby," Mom chokes out. "Sit, I'll get you some breakfast."

"I already did." Michael grins. "Dropped it off to

them a little earlier, and he was wrapped around her like a cobra."

"Aw," Samantha coos.

Kaleb laughs. "I knew you'd become all cuddly and shit once you finally got laid."

"Knock it off," my father warns, his tone sharp as he slaps the back of Kaleb's head.

Tilting my head, I take in his expression. My usually playful father is dead serious. His face is pale as he blinks the moisture back. "Well"—he clears his throat—"you just bring that little lady down whenever you're ready, son."

I nod my thanks.

"And no one go bothering them. Samantha, I'm talking to you."

My sister grins, rolling her eyes. When it's clear he wants an answer, she gives in quickly, "Fine, fine, I won't interrupt their love fest."

Wanting to get back to Charlotte, I head to the coffee pot and quickly pour two cups, conscious of already having been gone from her longer than I had hoped. She better not have even thought of touching that door.

I have barely finished pouring the second cup before a knock on the door sounds.

I freeze.

My hand stops midway to the coffee station, and my heart lodges in my throat. No one from town would come here unless it was an emergency . . . Like five dead trespassers at my family's campsite kind of emergency.

I try to calm myself down. It's not even been twelve hours, so the chances they've already been found are slim. I hear Sheriff McCallister greet my father.

Fuck. I'm going to have to kill the goddamn sheriff before I've had my morning coffee.

Like he can hear my thoughts, Michael gives me a small discreet shake of his head and a look that says calm the fuck down.

No one is taking my Charlotte; I don't care who I have to kill.

Standing, he joins me at the kitchen doorway, and together, we watch as our parents greet McCallister and his deputy.

"Sorry to bother you folks on a Saturday." McCallister apologizes, taking his hat off as he enters the house. His second-in-command follows him in. "You all know Deputy Cooper."

My father nods, shaking their hands.

"Would you boys like some coffee?" my mother offers.

Her words make my lips twitch as my father went to school with the sheriff. There is nothing boyish about him.

Kaleb nudges his way into the room from behind us, leaning his bulky body back on the wall beside me. "You take the sheriff, and Michael and I will take down Cooper before he gets a shot off."

My head snaps to him. "What?!"

He shrugs. "I've never heard you speak before or seen you smile." His face pulls into a deep frown. "Michael isn't the only one that'd do anything for you," Kaleb reminds me with a pointed look.

Our whispers go unnoticed as everyone but the three of us sit on the large sofas.

My eyes drift to the staircase, and adrenaline runs through me at the thought of what may come.

Ever the voice of reason, Michael hisses, "Easy, both of you." But even as he warns us, my little brother moves, striding until he reaches the bottom of the staircase. His lean body rests against the post like he doesn't have a care in the world. Like he couldn't kill both the officers before I finished my coffee. The one sitting on the kitchen counter going cold beside the cup I made for Charlotte.

And my anxiety spikes again. This is the first time I have left her alone, and while I don't think she would have run earlier had Michael not been there, I'm not entirely sure how convinced she is of the consequences should she try anything.

My clueless father smiles at his old classmate. "Not that I'm not happy to see you, Jeff, but everyone knows that if my family and I are here, it's to get away from our businesses and the town. What can I do for you?"

McCallister nods in the direction of my sister, who has decided to place herself a little too close to Cooper for my liking. My sister is not marrying a cop.

Over my dead body. Or better yet . . . his.

The smirk on Kaleb's face tells me he had the same thought.

"Perhaps the little ladies should go upstairs for this?"

Maybe killing a cop would be worth the heat, I think as my mothers' lips thin.

At my father's unimpressed look, the sheriff rushes on. "Seems you had some squatters up at the camp last night."

My feet shift to face toward the stairs, everything in me screaming to block the way. I force myself to take a deep breath. I trust Michael. No one is getting past him.

"You said we had squatters?" my father questions, placing a hand on my mother's knee.

The sheriff nods solemnly. "We got a call about there being lights on up there. The whole town knows about your family coming here for the holiday weekend, so I thought you'd stopped by on your way past," he continues, his words directed at my father.

"Have they made a mess?" my mother asks, clutching her neck. The quiver in her voice tells me she knows where this is going, but the two officers assume her worry is for the property, the same as my father does.

His hand squeezes her leg. They have always been an affectionate couple, something I failed to understand before now.

"Yeah, it was a mess," Cooper mutters to himself, earning a reprimanding glare from his boss.

"What Cooper means is that there's been . . . an accident of sorts," he explains, stumbling over his choice of words. "They were killed. College kids from Boise, five of them."

The noise my mother makes chips at my cold heart. Her cries muffle against my father's shirt, and he reaches out for Samantha, who quickly forgets about the useless cop beside her and hurries over into his arms.

"I'm sorry to have to inform you like this," he tells them, but his body language says he's anything but.

"We found some ID on them, and Delila already confirmed a few of them worked at the camp last summer."

Delila Masters has been running the camp for the past fifteen years, but she doesn't know anything that I need to worry about.

"One of the boys, Jason, was a particular pain in the ass. Her words." He chuckles. Delila is also the local preschool teacher, known for her patience with both children and adults. Her words speak volumes of the asshole that he was.

"We think one of them copied a key. Seems he's likely the culprit."

My dad nods. "Have the families been informed?"

"Yes, yes."

"We'll head down once the scene is released and clean the place up," Kaleb offers, trying to wrap things up. "Like it never happened," he promises, his words for my mother.

He may not have joined us this year, but he has in the past. Several times. Kaleb is a hunter, a master with a knife. But if there's no chase, there's no thrill in it for him.

"We actually came for two reasons," McCallister starts. "We saw that there was a fourth bed made up. Two couples and a single male were found. It sounds to reason that another person was there who may be our killer. Delila tells me that one of the deceased was always with another girl this summer." And there it is. He's fishing. "Charlie." The nickname makes my eye twitch.

"My brother's girl." Michael speaks up, motioning to where I stand. "Everyone knows about her. They've not hidden their relationship. And that good girl is definitely not a killer."

McCallister eyes me, but my brother talking for me is nothing new, so thankfully, he doesn't challenge it.

I don't think I could rein myself in and answer his fucking questions at the same time.

"I'm going to need to speak to her. Where is she?"

Absolutely fucking not.

I kick away from the wall, ready to add another body to my ever-growing count.

"She's sleeping," Mom rushes. "A migraine," she explains, a bit sheepish.

"She's a suspect," Cooper says, standing. Like

that'll fucking help him. He eyes me watching my feet as I take another step closer. Seems the weasel has grown a set of balls in the past five minutes.

"She's a young girl who has apparently just lost her friends," my father counters. Even clueless, he has my back. "Perhaps your chat can wait."

McCallister rubs at his chin. "Now would be best."

"Perhaps it can wait." He repeats, this time sterner.

"One of the boys, Dale, was beaten pretty badly, different than the others. Almost like it was personal."

I wonder if they'll have to do dental or DNA to confirm the prick's ID, seeing as he doesn't have a face anymore. I swallow down a smile.

"That's not a question," Kaleb states, always the smart-ass.

Cooper motions at my bare neck and chest. "Those are pretty big scratches."

"Again, not a question." The youngest Cromwell boy is getting pissed off.

"Besides, I think we can all guess where he got them. My brother may not talk, but his bedroom wall does. The banging went on late into the night." Michael winks. "Connecting walls. Thankfully, everyone else sleeps one floor below," he explains.

Mother makes a noise, not appreciating his crude words.

"Where were you boys last night?" the deputy asks.

Well, shit, he's not even trying to be discreet.

"Here," my mother snaps. "Daniel and Charlotte were in the outbuilding . . . Michael, too. All night. I saw them off to bed myself," she informs them, raising her chin.

"I'll need her to confirm, of course," he challenges while his boss sits there quietly.

A challenge which my mother rises too. "When she's ready."

"Gentlemen . . ." My father stands, his meaning clear. They've outstayed their welcome.

It's time for them to go.

Cooper opens his mouth to argue, but McCallister shuts him down quickly and quietly with one look. Our family owning half the town and the businesses that surround it comes in handy. After all, money talks.

McCallister smiles diplomatically. "I'm sure Deputy Cooper means nothing by it. He's just doing his job." He motions for Cooper to agree. "No one would suggest that a member of the town's founding family had anything to do with this." He swallows hard when my father's scowl doesn't lessen.

Unable to read the room or just not caring about the future of his job, Cooper snarks, "She's not a member of the family."

And just like that, Cooper seals his own fate.

Once outside, McCallister knocks his thumb against the side of his nose and clears his throat. "We, uhh, we will need to talk to her soon, Christopher."

"Mr. Cromwell," my father corrects, pleasantries have gone.

"Mr. Cromwell," he corrects himself. "Just to clear things up, of course." He rushes to add, desperate to make amends.

My father ignores him, along with the hand he holds out. Apparently, accusing two of his kids of multiple homicides is enough to make his shit list.

If only he knew.

I don't wait around for them to leave before I turn and head toward the stairs.

Michael gives me a look, which I know means he has my back. He'll settle shit down here, and we'll talk later. Well, he'll talk later.

Needing to get back to my girl, I quickly take the stairs two at a time.

CHAPTER TWENTY-ONE

Charlie

I force my eyes away from the closed door. I can't lay here and wait for him any longer. Daniel has been gone for twenty minutes, and although I'm unable to hear anything from the kitchen two floors below, something tells me that it'll be a while before he returns.

His warning rings through my head as I leave the bed, but the truth is, he didn't need to say the words aloud. I didn't want to leave. I hadn't even thought about it since I tried to crawl out of bed earlier, and even then, my effort was halfhearted.

Self-loathing rolls over me, and the need to wash it away is too strong to ignore.

The hot water is soothing, and I feel a sense of peace for the first time since Daniel left me alone.

I close my eyes and tilt my head back, enjoying how the heat seeps into my body and washes away my sins.

But it can't last forever, and the water eventually runs cold.

I leave the steam-filled bathroom, wrapping a towel around my chest. My eyes avoid the fogged mirror as I pass. The T-shirt from last night stays crumpled on the wet floor.

I want my things, my own clothes.

Splats sound when water drips off the end of my hair and onto the hardwood floors.

I can hear talking outside. Maybe it's Daniel?

Needing to know where he went, I walk to the window, and my heart drops. My stomach knots at what I see.

A police cruiser sits in the driveway. Do they know? Are they here for me?

I don't want to leave.

My eyes tear up at the thought, and I'm once again filled with self-loathing.

My soaked hair hangs in my face, and the water running off it thankfully hides my tears. I don't even know why I'm crying.

I should want this.

I stand at the window and try to look around outside. How many officers are there? Surely, there should be more?

They're leaving!

Two officers step off the porch, saying their good-byes. They head to their car quickly.

One of them waves his hand around, and he looks pissed. He's older, maybe mid-fifties. He jabs a finger back to where they were before hitting the roof of the car. The force of it makes water splash up.

The younger of the two looks up with a roll of his eyes, but they widen the minute he spots me.

My chest heaves. I reach out my hand, flattening my palm against the window. The pane is cold beneath my skin.

Suddenly, my body heats. The feel of bare skin touching my shoulders makes goosepimples spread down my arms.

Daniel.

His larger arm raises above me, and the officer below watches as Daniel grasps one of the curtains and pulls.

He kisses the crown of my head, making me forget about the officers.

I turn toward my tormentor, the man I want more than anything, just as he pulls the curtains closed, blocking out the men below and the real world that holds secrets and horrors that are easier to ignore within these four walls.

CHAPTER TWENTY-TWO

Charlie

I watch as my breath skitters across Daniel's naked chest. My finger runs over the bumps that soon follow.

His nipple hardens from my touch. I giggle when he playfully swats my ass.

I don't know how long we've lain here, but it's long enough for the sweat to have dried and the temperature to have dropped along with the sun.

I feel happy, my mind is empty, and a pleasant ache runs throughout my body, renewed from earlier.

After the officers left, Daniel explained that my friends had been found and that the police wanted to talk to me.

Panic filled me, but he was quick to distract me and make me forget.

Not that I had been in a rush to think about it.

Instead, I had begged and pleaded for more, for him to push me harder, to grip me tighter.

But now in the calmness of the evening, my mind betrays me.

My body rises as he takes a deep breath.

A gentle knock sounds seconds before the bedroom door opens just wide enough for Michael to squeeze inside.

Glancing down at where Daniel's wet cock lays on his leg, I feel my face blush and quickly tug the blanket up to cover his crotch and my hips.

Daniel's eyes remain closed, but a smirk plays at the edge of his lips, and his hand moves from where it had been resting on my ass, caressing its way to my breast where his hand possessively covers it, as if Michael hasn't already seen that and more.

He brought food again for the third time today. This time, it smells like lasagne. Yum. My mouth waters.

I try to sit up, but the hand on my chest turns painful as Daniel squeezes my breast.

"I think she's hungry, bro. Seems you worked up an appetite." Michael winks, settling into his seat from this morning.

Was it really just last night when I was brought here? It feels like days ago. But that's not surprising when it feels like I've known Daniel for a lifetime.

Why couldn't he be someone else? Anyone else.

I force the thoughts away, my new default setting.

Nothingness, numbness, peace.

Pulling the covers higher, I cover my nakedness until Daniel is satisfied enough to release me and let me sit up with the quilt tucked under my arms.

I give Michael a small grateful smile and edge the food tray closer. "It smells amazing."

He shrugs casually. "When no one came down for dinner, I offered to bring it up. Besides" — his brow arches — "Mom was going to bring it up."

Daniel chokes on a bite of food, coughing as I quickly pass him the glass of water.

"Careful," I warn. "Small sips."

I can hear Michael laugh, but I only have eyes for Daniel. His face is red from coughing, but his expression has softened. The way he looks at me makes my heart swell and my soul melt. He's not used to being taken care of.

Why couldn't we meet differently?

Why did he have to be a killer?

My eyes drift closed when he presses a kiss to my forehead.

"As cute as this is, we need to talk about McCallister. What do you want to do?"

Daniel pulls back from me long enough to fill his fork once more. Lifting it to my mouth in offering, he waits for me to take it.

"Plan." Daniel's voice is as rough as always, deep and penetrating.

Michael nods. "Agreed, we stick to the plan. We knew they'd find the bodies. It's just sooner than we thought."

I take another bite of food and try not to listen, but it's impossible.

"Mom won't say anything. She'll stick to us being here all night and the cameras at the main road will confirm it since we went in another way."

Daniel grunts in acknowledgment.

Pain ricochets through my chest at what the police found. Of what Michael and Daniel did.

The two of them talk back and forth. Michael makes suggestions, and Daniel grunts at any he approves of.

They decide that their alibis are secured because of their family, and that with no evidence, the sheriff's department will start looking elsewhere soon.

Worst case, they'll take care of the sheriff. My throat closes at the suggestion.

Someone else can't die because of me.

"I'll go," I whisper.

Silence greets my words.

Thinking they didn't hear me, I clear my throat and repeat it. "I'll go. I'll tell the police I was here with you and that Dale and I fought." No one speaks, so I rush on. "I'll tell the sheriff we broke up. Then I'll go home, and I won't tell anyone. I swear." I whisper the last two words like a plea.

The panic at someone else being killed grows tenfold at my offer to leave, and I refuse to analyze my body's reaction. The same way I have refused to think about any other reaction I have had around him in the past two days.

My heart thumps as I think for a moment that Daniel is actually considering my suggestion. And then I see his face.

If fury were a man, he'd be sitting next to me.

Violence vibrates out of him.

Slowly, as if he is trying to contain himself, Daniel's head turns to me.

"Repeat it."

I don't want to. I swallow the words and shake my head quickly, whipping my loose hair back and forth.

His large frame unravels, and he looms over me. Walking around the end of the bed, he braces himself on the wooden frame.

"Repeat what you just said."

I think I'm really having a heart attack this time.

My fingers grip my chest, and I feel sick as I force the words out of my mouth.

"I could leave." My voice is weak. "It will take suspicion off," I explain, wanting him to know it would be for him.

His arm snaps out, his hand wrapping around my neck before I can even blink.

"You are never leaving." His grip is tight but not painful. Enough to remind me who is in charge . . . like I need it.

"I'm sorry." I am, for many things.

Letting me go, Daniel stands tall, his chest heaving as he claws in more air.

"That is my bed you're sitting in, my cum that

drips out of your pussy." His words are laced with disgust, and it's the worst pain I have ever felt.

"I'm sorry," I repeat. I need him to believe me.

He ignores me and steps into a pair of sweatpants. His movements are stiff and forced.

But he doesn't speak to me again and motions for Michael to leave. I scramble off the bed when Daniel goes to follow him.

Crying, I rush to the door, banging as he secures it behind him without so much as a look in my direction.

I hit the locked door a few more times before my body wracks from my sobs.

Slumping to the floor naked, I cry for what I have just done, the peace between us that I ruined, and for the lives lost just the day before.

CHAPTER TWENTY-THREE

Charlie

He hates me. The same words echo around my head, my inner voice taking a break from telling me what a bitch I am.

Daniel has been kind and giving to me no matter what he did. But now I ruined it. And for what? I hadn't meant the words, even as I said them.

I wipe at my face, my tears never-ending.

Lying on the crumpled bedding, I strain to hear anything from the floors below.

He never came back, not even to sleep. I've been stuck in this room for almost a day with nothing but my thoughts for company. My skin is itching for me to get out. Michael brought food in this morning, but I didn't even move. My limbs feel heavy, and I'm uninterested in food. Always a first.

Something Michael was not happy about when he saw the food untouched at dinnertime. Switching the plates out, he had uttered a few words of how I needed to eat.

I hadn't. I'm still lying in the same place, my mind racing with questions of whether Daniel still needs me or if he even still wants me.

The bedroom door opens, but I ignore it, thinking it's Michael with more food.

My eyes fly open as the bed dips behind me. A smell surrounds me, his smell. Wood, earthy, and spice.

Daniel.

Soft kisses caress my thigh, and my breath hitches. Teeth sink into the round of my ass cheek. A sob escapes me when his lips kiss the small of my back and continue to the nape of my neck.

"No leaving." He's not asking, but I answer anyway.

"Yes, sir."

"Good girl."

I shiver at the praise; he owns me with those words.

Pushing up onto my hands and knees, I turn, needing to see his face.

"I didn't mean it," I rush, trying to reassure him. My voice cracks. "I want to stay with you. I promise."

His hands rub at my naked back, our fronts plastered together.

Daniel hums, trying to soothe me, his hands stroking from my hair to my ass.

It works. Within minutes, he calms my body.

I whimper as he pulls away, but a kiss to my nose quickly soothes me.

"If you ever try to leave again, I will not leave you alone in the room as punishment." I frown. That's a terrible threat because I don't want him to leave. "I will stay and punish you. Do you understand?"

I agree quickly. "Yes, sir."

One solid nod lets me know I'm forgiven before he climbs from the bed.

"Eat, then change. My brothers are waiting," he orders, lifting the food tray next to me. Chicken and rice.

It's cold and looks unappetizing, but I have never wanted to follow an order more. Lifting a forkful of rice, I make sure he's watching as I put it in my mouth. His smile spreads warmth through me until it settles and grows in my chest.

I rush to eat the food, and after a few warnings to slow down, Daniel takes the fork from me, feeding me bite-sized pieces until the plate is cleared.

"Good girl." He rewards me with another kiss on my nose.

I beam at him, happy he's pleased.

I dress quickly, thankfully into my own clothes from my weekend bag, minus a bra.

My nipples pebble and brush against the wool of my sweater at the thought of why he wouldn't give me one. The memory of the outhouse table makes me blush just as we meet his brothers at the steps of the cabin porch.

Hand in hand, we follow his brothers as we all walk toward the forest.

The grounds really are beautiful. I could see from the window that the trees lining both sides of the long winding drive are tall and thick. But as we cross the drive and walk into the trees, the sheer size of the lake that the house sits on the edge of really registers. It has to be the same lake the camp sits on.

It's quiet here. Peaceful, almost otherworldly.

The three brothers walk in silence, one that says they are used to it. The new man is tall but shorter than Michael and Daniel. He's lean and sporty with a runner's body, but unlike his brothers, he has light hair.

He and Michael walk ahead, but he keeps peeking back every few minutes, his gaze glued to where Daniel has linked our hands.

"Kaleb," Daniel tells me, motioning to his brother.

Kaleb grins. "Holy fuck."

"Takes some getting used to," Michael tells him, slapping his little brother on the shoulder.

Confused, I look up at Daniel, who simply shrugs.

We keep walking at a steady pace. Daniel is happy for us to hang back while Kaleb and Michael playfully shove at each other, occasionally adding us in on their banter. But for the most part, Daniel and I walk in silence because words are not needed.

We stick to a well-worn path for around twenty minutes before veering off into the trees. Empty branches dominate the sky, blocking out some of the wind. Crispy leaves crunch under his heavy boots.

By the time we reach our destination, my feet ache. Something sharp stabs at my heel. My sneakers were not made for traipsing through the woods and have let more than one stone inside.

I try to pull my hand away, but Daniel is reluctant. I point toward a fallen log, showing him where I want to go.

Instead of releasing me, he escorts me over and brushes debris off the top, knocking away as much dirt as he can.

"Thanks," I whisper with a smile.

Messing with my shoe, I sigh as I'm forced to take it off and shake it. I grin as the stones drop to the forest floor.

Focused on refitting my shoe, I ignore the brothers talking. Michael and Kaleb chat while Daniel stands over me, watching my every move. His eye twitches with every stone that falls out.

"You should have said, little one." He's upset.

I don't know what to say, unsure how to express my thoughts. "I guess I didn't want to disrupt our truce." I shrug.

Daniel's face softens. His fingers grasp my chin. "You and I, we don't need a truce. We just work."

I give him a watery smile. My sweet man is back.

"Can she see?" Kaleb asks, interrupting our locked gaze.

I look away at the question to see Kaleb holding out a set of binoculars toward me. I can't see Daniel's quiet reply, but I feel it when the hands on my shoulders squeeze in approval.

Taking the proffered binoculars, I peer in.

It's the camp, and we're behind the counselor's cabin.

We must be standing on a hill not far behind the campgrounds.

I watch as police officers mill around. Looking among them, I realize that the shorter one passing out coffee is one of the men who came to the cabin yesterday, the younger one.

"Cooper tried to corner me in town this morning," Kaleb says.

Michael clicks his tongue in disapproval. "Didn't you go with Dad?"

"Yeah." He laughs. "He was furious. Hence why a deputy is babysitting the crime scene."

"Plan," Daniel grunts.

I bite my lip at the sound.

Michael nods. "Daniel's right, we stick to the plan . . . for now." He heaves a sigh. "She'll have to talk to them at some point, Daniel."

I feel a puff of air on the top of my head, a sign of his frustration.

"My offer to kill the deputy is still there," Kaleb offers casually. Too casually.

He hasn't even lifted his head out of his own binoculars when he spoke, like it was an everyday thing. That's when I realized . . . it is.

He is one of them, three peas in a pod. Kaleb is a killer, too.

"Easy," Michael warns, pointing a finger at both of them. "Once a year, that's the deal. Any more than that, and we'd get caught. We don't change what works."

"My bad," Kaleb acknowledges, lifting a hand in apology. "I should have come this year, but it didn't sound as exciting, which was clearly a mistake. Next year, pick someone who's going to run, please?"

I feel sick. Bending, I try to drag air into my lungs. A solid force pushes my head down farther until it hangs between my knees.

"Deep breaths, good girl."

And just like that, my heart stops racing, and my chest rises with deep breaths. My body eager to follow his instructions.

We sit there for hours, watching and waiting as the campground is cleared out. The brothers observing and joking.

My stomach rumbles, and Daniel immediately stands, his face drawn with worry.

"That would be those meals you didn't eat," Michael reprimands from where he sits against a thick tree next to us, his disapproval clear.

I smile sheepishly, but he reaches out to knock me under the chin to show he's not truly angry.

My wince as we start walking does not go unnoticed. The hand in my own quickly pulls me to a stop.

Daniel raises a single brow in question.

"The stones in my shoe were in there for a while, and now my sole hurts," I say, embarrassed. "I'll be okay," I reassure quickly.

I let out a quick squeak when I'm suddenly lifted under my arms and placed on the log we were just sitting on.

I watch my eyes widen as Daniel turns and motions for me to climb onto his back. *He's kidding, right?* Too stunned, I just stand there and stare.

He straightens and turns to me. "Climb on," he orders, giving me his back again and tapping his shoulder.

And as it has been since we met, my body listens to him without question. I loop my arms around his neck, wrap my legs around his waist, and hold on. A smile tugs at my mouth the whole way back.

We reach the end of the tree line much quicker than we had going. I guess my small strides had slowed them the first time. Appreciation runs through me as neither of his brothers had complained about the slower pace.

Noise greets us, and an older-looking man grins at us over the top of his car.

"Well, hello." His wide smile is from ear to ear as he waves.

Daniel tenses under me.

I give a small wave back.

"Daniel, come help your old man."

Gently, Daniel crouches so that he can set me down safely.

I unwrap myself from his waist. "Thanks," I whisper, grateful for the lift.

I look up at him in worry, but I needn't have. A tightening of his hand around mine along with a kiss to my head, and Daniel silently strides over to his father.

His mom and a woman around my age, maybe a little younger, smile, waving when they meet my gaze. I give an awkward smile back, unsure of how to act.

Daniel remains calm as he walks over to the car, but my heart is in my throat. Kaleb runs over to help. He peeks back at me, probably to check where I might go.

Michael comes to stand beside me, his voice low. "Remember what I said, Charlie. I'll do anything for Daniel." I look at him, confused. "You have a family, right?" I nod and wait for him to continue, but he doesn't. He doesn't need to because the threat is clear, and he must think so too as with those words, he walks off toward where his dad and brothers are unloading the trunk.

CHAPTER TWENTY-FOUR

Charlie

Loud cheers sound around the dining room table as Sam whines about her brother's teasing.

My giggle joins the noise as I grin at Daniel. His hand squeezes the back of my neck firmer, and my stomach flutters at his smile.

"Whatever. You asses owe me for taking Charlie hiking and leaving me out," she complains again with a pout.

Helen tuts.

"Language," Christopher reprimands his daughter.

Kaleb laughs, taunting his sister more.

They're so normal that I find myself forgetting everything that has happened. They are just one big, loud family full of love and laughter.

I wish things were different, that Daniel had asked me on a date at the gas station and we had gone out for dinner, had frantic sex in the cab of his truck, and maybe then we could be having dinner with his family without the unspoken words hanging between us.

Daniel has been on edge ever since we left the woods and I met the rest of his family. Like he expects me to scream and demand my freedom at any minute.

The fact that I haven't makes me hate myself even more.

The food has been delicious. His mother really knows how to cook. I eye the last of the potatoes, hoping to mop up my gravy with them. My eyes battle with Kaleb's, a smile playing on our lips, and we both reach for the pot. We grab hold at the same time and playfully glare at one another.

"Hey, hey. Guests first." Helen smiles.

"I'm a growing boy! It's not my fault she could eat a horse," Kaleb sasses.

A loud clatter startles us all, and Kaleb's chair tilts onto the back legs, causing him to let go of the dish and flail before the chair quickly slams back down onto all four legs. Everyone laughs.

A large hand covers my own, lifting the potatoes and placing them next to my plate.

I watch with wide eyes as Daniel winks down at me. Leaning in, he places a sweet and gentle kiss on my lips, motioning for me to eat. Then he sits back, looking at his youngest brother as if daring him to even try something.

My face heats, and the other ladies at the table melt.

"You're a good boy, Daniel," his mother whispers.

"Aw, Dan Dan. You're so cute!"

"Don't ever call me that again."

"Dan Dan," I whisper, earning myself a poke in the ribs. Not pleased when I laugh, Daniel leans down and bites my neck, his teeth latching onto my skin in full view of his family. My face flames.

"Movie night!" Sam demands, thankfully taking everyone's eyes off us, clapping as she stands.

Everyone either agrees quickly or groans like they know it is inevitable.

"Fine, but not a fucking rom-com. Horror, it is Halloween after all," Michael tells her.

CHAPTER TWENTY-FIVE

Daniel

My knee twitches, and I have to remind myself to calm the fuck down.

So much for bringing Charlotte down to meet my family when I was ready. Rolling my eyes, I peek back into the kitchen, where my girl stands with my mom and sister preparing snacks.

Friday the 13th remains paused on the television. Samantha made it around thirty minutes in before she got so scared that she needed a break. Of course, she didn't say that. No, she went with needing a snack despite eating a full meal not even an hour earlier.

My father should have known better than to close the curtains and dim the lights. We all know what my sister is like watching a scary movie at this time of night. But it's not my bed she will be crawling into for comfort. At nineteen, it is something that she still hasn't grown out of, and according to our dad, the reason we do not have any more siblings.

Of course, we know that is not true, nor is it something he would ever put a stop to, no matter how old she gets. Being the baby and the only girl in the family has its perks.

Kaleb hasn't fucking helped by talking about how he agreed with Jason and that they all deserved it. Our father laughed, but Mother, not so much, which is why she had been more than happy to make nachos.

I smile at the thought of my sister being scared, given who was in the room with her. Samantha couldn't be in a safer house. Even if someone managed to get past my brothers and me, my father would lay down his life for her. Not that he'd need to.

I know Michael has been praying for a home invasion for years, someone to justifiably kill between our yearly hunts, and while I would normally agree, the thought of someone in my home, in Charlotte's and my home, fills me with fear more than rage.

Usually one to avoid these movie nights, I find myself grateful and hopeful for the future. Charlotte had been quick to curl up against me, her head buried in my neck when the killing started.

I had watched the beginning of the film with my girl in my arms and a smile on my face. It was perfect, but now she's hidden away in the kitchen, and my mind won't stop racing with what-ifs.

Samantha skips into the room, happily chewing on a corn chip smothered in salsa.

"Ready to continue?" Dad asks.

"Mm-hmm." She nods, but we've lost her to the nachos. She won't even notice when the film has been put back on.

"Come on, ladies. We're about to restart the film," my father calls out.

Something clangs in the kitchen, but no one answers.

I lean more to the right, trying to see Charlotte, and my anxiety rises more when I can't sneak a look.

I don't last more than a few minutes before rising.

They both stand at the island, plating the last of the corn chips into a giant bowl. Something is off. Charlotte's breaths are deep, and she's blinking quickly.

"Hi, baby." My mom smiles, but it's weak. When she bites the corner of her lip, I frown, looking back and forth between my two most important women.

Charlotte smiles softly as she walks past, carrying the salsa.

"Can you take these, please," my mom asks, holding out the chips.

I nod, moving forward to take the bowl. Just as my fingers touch it, my mother whispers, her voice barely noticeable, but I do hear her, and my blood turns to ice. "She asked me to help."

My head snaps up.

"Help her leave," she continues.

I clench my eyes closed, and the breath twists out of my lungs.

"I will sort it."

Her chin quivers. She hates this. It's too much to ask, and I know that. But I can't give Charlotte up. I won't.

I had hoped overnight isolation would work, that our pull was strong enough. Charlotte's reaction when I returned to her this afternoon had given me hope, made me believe that she wanted me just as much as I did her.

Apparently not. It's time to fix that.

A heavy sigh escapes me, but excitement runs through me at the thought of how my night is about to change.

I brush the blond hair away from my mom's face, kissing the top of her head. Her arms wrap around me, and I quickly return the hug, something I've never done before.

"I will fix this," I promise.

Her hand tightens on the back of my shirt.

"I will love her enough," I swear.

Her head rubs against my shirt as she nods, knowing I will not break my word.

I watch as she leaves the kitchen, then pick up the chips. Just as I approach the door, the vegetable rack catches my eye. Swerving to the right I quickly grab the top item and shove it into my pocket.

CHAPTER TWENTY-SIX

Charlie

Fuck!

My hands shake as I place the bowl down. What had I been thinking?

We were having a good night. I was having a good night.

Sam had left the kitchen, and the words just came out. Helen knows. I thought she would help me, but she had ignored me and acted as if I hadn't spoken. Then Daniel had come in, and I couldn't take the words back.

And God, did I want to. As soon as the words were out there, I wanted to take them back, just like yesterday.

Now he was alone with his mother while I sat

here, my gut clenching, not knowing if she would tell. And I can do nothing but wait.

I don't have to wait for long.

The knots in my stomach drop to my feet, taking all my blood with them as my face drains.

"Son?" Christopher asks, seeing him in the doorway.

"Bedtime." One word is all he says.

"Aw," Sam complains, pouting. "The film," she insists, pointing at the television.

"Charlotte, bedtime." His voice is calm and collected, but I see his cheek twitch with impatience.

I rush to my feet. "Thank you for today, everyone. Tonight was fun." I lean down and hug Sam, stopping her protests.

I want Helen to know I'm not mad and understand her loyalty to her son. So, I reach over and embrace her, too. She kisses my cheek, rubbing my back.

"Good night, sweet girl," she whispers, stroking my cheek as we part.

"What about me?" Kaleb laughs with his arms wide open.

"I fucking dare you."

Daniel's words only make him laugh harder.

Michael shakes his head. "One day, he's going to punch you in the neck, and we're not going to be shocked, baby brother."

Their playfulness helps to calm my nerves and steady my breaths as I take Daniel's outstretched hand, letting him link our fingers as he leads me up the stairs.

I don't fight him like I won't fight what's coming. I deserve it.

By the time we reach our bedroom, my hands are sweaty, and my body shakes.

"For what it's worth, I'm sorry, Daniel. I didn't mean it."

The bedroom door closes behind us, shutting out the rest of the family.

Daniel doesn't speak at first, stripping out of his clothes in silence. I perch on the edge of the bed, waiting for him to tell me what to do.

I strain my ears, trying to follow him through the room as he shuffles around, disrobing.

"Strip and climb onto the bed."

I jump to my feet at the order, eager to please.

I need this, just as he does.

My sweater goes quickly. I turn to find him. I need to see his face, show him I can be his good girl. I have to know what he's thinking.

All thoughts of why I turned flee the minute I see him. Naked and glorious.

The man is phenomenal, and I will never get enough.

Looking at him now, standing here looking at me like I am his whole world, I know in my heart that I will never leave him, not of my own accord.

"I was not unclear." His words bring me out of my thoughts, and his strict voice makes my body react. A reaction that only grows tenfold when his hand wraps around my throat. "Strip and get on the bed." He speaks slowly, his words as defined as his abs.

His hand doesn't release me. Instead, we stand still with our eyes locked as I unbutton my jeans and shove them down as far as I can without bending. With my movement restricted, I'm forced to lift my legs, pulling awkwardly until I can stomp out of my pants and kick them to the side along with my shoes.

Naked, I grin at him in triumph.

A chuckle rumbles out of his wide chest, and my eyes draw down, taking him in. His chest is scattered with dark hair, his abs so defined they could have been carved, a trail of dark hair teases from below his belly button down to where it frames his huge erection. His cock stands high, aiming straight at me, the head an angry red color.

My mouth waters with want.

He uses his thumb to tilt my head back until we are eye to eye once more.

"Bed. Head down, ass up."

"Yes, sir."

Daniel watches as I climb up onto the bed on my hands and knees. Pointing, he directs me to face the headboard.

I don't want to. I want to see him.

Licking my lips, I hesitate.

Daniel doesn't speak again. He just tilts his head, and it's enough to tell me to do as I'm told.

Pouting, I turn. The white of the wall is not nearly as fulfilling to look at as his naked body. I drop to my forearms dramatically, not even trying to hide my annoyance.

"Ahh." My body rocks when a hand connects with my ass.

"You're in enough trouble."

I nod, panting.

My head drops to the bed, my hands fisting the covers. The wait is killing me.

I turn my head, looking back at where he stands at the bathroom counter. I squint, trying to see what he's doing.

He's holding something in his left hand. It's a weird shape, and I can't tell what it is. I watch as Daniel's right hand picks up a second object that flicks open in his hand. A knife.

What is he doing?

Steadily, he scrapes at the second object, peels it, cutting it.

What the fuck is that?

Daniel steps toward the bed, and I know I'm about to find out. My whole body shakes with excitement, liquid heat runs through me.

Arousal coats my inner thighs.

The cover twists in my hands. The sound of Daniel's excited breaths join mine as he climbs onto the bed behind me, placing something on the sheets beside my head.

Ginger.

I frown, wondering what it's for. Why would he peel and cut that, now of all times?

I moan as his hands grasp my ass, squeezing my cheeks. I feel as his wet tongue grazes my forbidden hole.

I gasp, trying to push up.

"Daniel," I plead, but I have no idea what I want, what I'm begging for.

He doesn't answer. Instead, I feel something press against my asshole. It takes me a minute to realize that it's the ginger, but the minute I do, I shift forward, trying to move away.

I don't get far before wide hands grip my hips and tug me back to where I was.

My face flames when my cheeks are pulled wide, the sound of spitting tells me what just landed on my hole. Daniel presses the ginger in quickly. He's not gentle as he forces it inside.

I wiggle my hips at the foreign feeling. It's small and short, not reaching in very far, but the thickness makes me sting.

My moan rings out as Daniel presses his hips forward, his thick cock penetrating my pussy just as the ginger fills my ass.

He rotates the ginger left to right, pulling it almost completely out, then thrusting it back in. Back and forth. He tugs the ginger, matching the rhythm with the thrusts of his cock.

A hand on my shoulder pulls me back onto him as he thrusts forward.

The sound of our joining echoes around the room.

"Uhhhh." I don't recognize the noises leaving me. I feel full.

"Fuck, fuck, fuck."

His thrusts are hard, harder than ever before, almost mean.

And I fucking love it. I feel myself build. My body grips him tighter, and then it happens.

A heat like I have never felt before explodes in my ass. The ginger burns.

I launch myself forward, but Daniel follows, his body staying buried inside mine. He lands on top of me as I lay spread out flat on the bed, his weight shoving the ginger in deep as he follows, his hips bouncing off mine while he keeps himself buried in my pussy. My ass continues to contract, squeezing tight. It feels wet like its softening within the grip of my body.

Every slam of Daniel's hips causes the ginger to shove farther inside and rub against my sphincter. An orgasm builds beyond a level I have yet to feel. I feel a fullness in both places that somehow seems to gather in my womb.

I cry out as it peaks, but it's suddenly gone. Daniel pulls himself away, his cock slipping out of me, and I am left on the edge of a cliff, all burning throbs and aching ring.

The man behind me flips me. My chest heaves as I stare up at him.

"Please," I beg. I need him so much.

His body lays over mine, and I eagerly spread my legs, inviting him back inside. An invitation that he wastes no time in accepting. His lips meet mine. It's sloppy and desperate as we both chase our high.

Daniel pulls my thighs higher on his waist, his nails digging into my skin.

The sound of our bodies meeting, the smell of sex, and the feeling of his balls slapping against the ginger all add to what I'm feeling, and I quickly find myself on the edge again.

My pussy burns, and I realize some of the juice from the ginger has worked its way inside.

I peer up at Daniel as my hands grip his broad shoulders, fearing he'll pull out again. His face is flushed, more than when we usually do this. He feels the ginger, too.

My eyes screw shut, the knowledge that I am not the only one feeling the heat, that the cock ramming inside me is coated with the essence of ginger, pushes me over the edge, and I scream just as I am about to step off that cliff.

But then it stops short. My eyes fly open, and I gasp for air. His large hand is wrapped around my throat again, only this time tighter.

"Bad girls do not come." He breathes against my lips, his hips starting quick, short thrusts that never once slow.

I reach up to scratch at his hands while digging my heels into his ass, silently asking for what I need.

"No," he growls, denying me.

His hips pump a few more times before he shoves himself as far into me as he can, roaring out his release.

His hips grind, and I feel his release stream into me, overflowing and dripping beneath me.

Just when I think I can't take anymore. Daniel removes his hand. I suck in big gulps of air filling my lungs desperately.

My nethers throb. I need just the slightest of touch, and I know I will fly.

"I said no." Daniel pants, his face just above mine.

He pulls out of me, careful not to graze my clit. His hands are gentle as he turns me to the side, pushes my legs until they are bent, and spreads my ass cheeks.

"No," I whine, my word ending on a sob as he removes the ginger.

My body thumps with excitement, and the feeling of being on edge doesn't leave me.

I lay there with Daniel's large body looming over me, boxing me in. When I realize that he will, in fact, leave me like this, anger and guilt build in my chest.

After all, I caused this.

The first sob is quiet, muffled by the bedding. The second is louder, stronger, and earns me a kiss on my shoulder.

My sobs grow, coming quicker and stronger, each one earning me another kiss until, eventually, Daniel lays me out so he can lay his body over mine, sandwiching me between himself and the bed.

I let his weight seep in. The pulse between my legs and the burn in my ass recede after a while, and slowly, my eyes drop.

A hand combs through my hair.

"Sleep, Charlotte. You will need your rest. You're not my good girl again, just yet."

CHAPTER TWENTY-SEVEN

Charlie

Last night was . . . different. Exciting and painful. Everything and nothing.

My body hummed throughout the night, waking me in intervals. Daniel was right there to deny me each time I shifted with need.

His hand slapped away mine when I tried to sneak it down the front of my body, and his leg pried mine apart to deny me any friction.

This morning, I'm tired, horny, and very, very sorry.

But he'll forgive me when he comes back. Hope and excitement bloom in my chest, and heat fills my pulsing crotch.

I turn my head, pressing my cheek into the pillow,

and moan. The sound is muffled by the panties Daniel placed in my mouth.

I rock my hips, but even when he's not in the room, Daniel controls my pleasure.

We woke tangled, his body still stretched over mine. My body shivers at the memory of his stern eyes watching me, tracking me as I used the bathroom first thing. The way his face was shrouded in mischief made his enjoyment clear.

I almost cried when his father called requesting help to load his truck in town, something about staying at the cabin for an extra few days and Christopher needing help restocking supplies.

Emotion had been clear in his father's voice when Daniel agreed to meet, making me think it was something else. He wants to see his son.

So I put on a brave face and promised to be a good girl, his good girl, while he was out. My words were met with a smirk and a glint that told me I would not like what happened next.

And I haven't, at least that is what I keep repeating to myself as I lie here spread open, wanting and waiting.

"Do this and be my good girl again." He whispered those words into my ear as the final rope was tightened around my wrist.

The air was cool; a small fire had warmed us through the night, but Daniel had extinguished it on his way out, not wanting to leave it unsupervised. He promised to return before I got too cold.

My nipples bead painfully, and while the room is cool, I know the room temperature isn't the sole reason. My body hasn't calmed from last night. The sex was phenomenal, painful, and arousing beyond my belief, but I needed that relief, even if I had to beg him when he returned.

The speech I could give runs through my head when I hear it . . . voices.

Someone is on this floor. No, people—more than one—and they are heading right this way. My stomach drops, and my heart stops. Holy fuck.

I tug on my restraints desperately, but the rope holds tight on my wrists and ankles. The bedposts creak in protest of my struggles.

Fuck!

"I don't know why you need to talk to her now," Sam says, confused.

I hear them stop walking. "Are you sure your brothers aren't here?" a man asks.

"I told you he's in town helping my dad. I don't know where Michael and Kaleb went." I can practically hear the sound of her rolling her eyes. "You can ask my mom. She'll be back any second."

"No, no," he rushes. "I'll just talk to her now."

I strain to hear more.

"So she's stayed up here all weekend?"

"I guess, except for last night." Sam sounds unsure, and I lie here praying she'll take him back downstairs. "But they're a couple, and my brother's private anyway, plus her friends just died."

They're outside the door now, and I don't fight the tears of humiliation as they run freely down my face.

I'm naked, gagged, and tied to her brother's bed. She cannot see this. I would have to ask Michael to actually kill me. The thought sounds better and better with every beat of my heart.

I tug frantically at my bound wrists as I'm forced to lie here and helplessly watch the doorknob turn.

My heart cracks at the same time the door begins to open.

"What the fuck do you think you're doing?"

Holy fuck.

I have never been so pleased to hear someone's voice. Michael is angry, his tone is one of outrage.

"Samantha, you know better. Anyone's room is off-limits without permission."

My head flops back on my pillow, and I breathe for what feels like the first time since Sam and the man stepped onto the landing.

"And you, Deputy Fuckface"—*Kaleb?*—"are not welcome in this house."

Yes, definitely Kaleb, and he's even more furious than Michael.

The door slams closed, causing my whole body to sink into the bed. Relief courses through me, fear having chased away any sense of arousal.

"Our father won't be happy," Michael warns him, but the man scoffs, clearly not worried, "And neither am I."

I flinch, wondering if the man just signed his own death warrant.

"Go to your room, Samantha," Kaleb orders.

"No! You're not my dad."

"Clearly, because if I was your daddy, you wouldn't sit well for the next few days. Now, I will not tell you again." Kaleb's deep voice is loud, and I wonder if he closed the door. Is he standing in front of it, guarding me? "Go to your room."

Sam sniffles. "I was just trying to help." Her retreating steps are quick as she runs down the stairs.

"Get the fuck out of my house," Michael orders.

"I thought it was your father's house, but then again, he isn't really your father, is he? You're both little bastards."

What?

Anger fills me at his words. How dare he say something like that. Even if it's somehow true, Christopher clearly loves those men.

The need to defend them surprises me. I hardly know Kaleb and Michael . . . well, I know more than I should.

Footsteps lead away, but I can't tell who by that alone.

"I really wanna kill that motherfucker," Kaleb whispers.

"I know."

"Next year?" Kaleb asks hopefully.

"After that comment? You bet, little brother."

A knock sounds on the bedroom door. "Charlie?"

"Mhh," I sound out, unable to answer.

Michael chuckles in response. "Daniel will be home soon. You okay?"

"Uh-huh." I try to answer loud enough so that they won't come in.

"Good girl. He won't be long."

Good girl. The words bounce around my head over and over.

Kaleb laughs. "He'll be even quicker when he hears about this. Now who's going to deal with Samantha before Dad comes back and coddles her?"

The sound of their talking dims as they move away. My thoughts turn to Sam and what punishment she may have just earned herself. But honestly, I can't find it in myself to care, not when I was seconds away from having half of Daniel's family see me at my most vulnerable.

I sigh in relief again and pray that Daniel returns quickly.

CHAPTER TWENTY-EIGHT

Charlie

My relief at seeing Daniel doesn't last long.

He had kissed my wrists and ankles as he untied me, his actions sweet and his touch gentle, but talk soon turned to the man who had come to the house; Deputy Cooper. Although I think I prefer Kaleb's name for him, Deputy Fuckface.

I giggle, causing Daniel to turn his head away from the road in front of us.

"Deputy Fuckface," I explain with another giggle.

He chuckles with me, his fingers grazing my cheeks that heat at having his whole attention. His hand joins mine, resting on my thigh.

"Remember," he prompts, squeezing my hand.

I nod, eager not to disappoint him. I like being his good girl.

"I'll tell them what you and Michael agreed on. We've been dating since this summer, when I first met you." I recite the story I now have engraved into my brain. Hours of it being repeated will do that to you. "Love at first sight," I add, the words that are my own. The best lies are mixed with the truth, or so my grandmother says. "I didn't know about their plan to squat at the camp. I just caught a ride down here, where I planned to spend the weekend with you. When we were leaving our dorm, they mentioned the camp."

Daniel smiles his approval, and my heart skips a beat.

"You met me at Duke's gas station Friday morning, then my friends and I went our separate ways." I press on, trying not to think about the fact that I have only known Daniel for three days. "I was at the cabin in the afternoon but only for about an hour, and that was only to tell them they needed to leave." This weekend has been both the worst and the best days of my life. How fucked up is that?

"And," he encouraged.

I blink at him, trying to remember anything I had forgotten. "Both you and Michael collected me before we went back to Duke's to pay after I learned my friends ditched the tab. You didn't call the police about them squatting because they were my friends, and they had agreed to leave in the morning. Due to their drinking, you agreed it was the safest option."

Daniel raises our hands, kissing the back of mine. "That's my good girl."

I beam at him.

"We're here," he announces, pulling the car onto the lot.

Together, we walk into the station. Sheriff McCallister jumps to his feet as soon as he sees us.

"Th-Thank you for coming down." The sheriff stutters, "I appreciate your family's understanding over our earlier mishap."

A man I assume to be Deputy Cooper glares at us from where he sits at his desk.

Daniel smirks at him. "Deputy."

"Officer, actually," the sheriff corrects. Well, that would explain the death glares.

I look at Daniel for confirmation, and he nods that he and his family are responsible.

The sheriff rubs his chin. "Well, we'll make this as quick as we can. Let's go to my office and talk, shall we, Charlie?"

Taking a deep breath, I straighten my back and follow him, leaving Daniel waiting for me by the desks.

You got this, Charlie.

CHAPTER TWENTY-NINE

Daniel

Pride runs through me. Charlotte did great.

Of course, she did. My girl was made for this, for me.

The sheriff ate everything up. Cooper not so much, but his demotion means he's less of a threat, and with his livelihood on the line, the inquisitive little shit will be more careful.

I turn onto the road leading out of town, itching to get back to the cabin where my family waits.

Charlotte has changed everything in such a small time. Never before have I felt the need to rush home to be with my family.

I smile, knowing Charlotte is now included in that. *My family.* A thrill goes through me at the thought of Charlotte helping me to add more members to it.

My hand runs up her leg beneath her dress, settling on her inner thigh.

I have never been prouder of anyone, not even Michael.

My good girl.

The need to show her is overwhelming, and after that performance, she has more than earned her reward.

We have only been on the main road for a few minutes before Duke's comes into view. Signaling, I turn onto the parking lot, driving past the gas pumps.

Charlotte frowns. "Do we need gas?"

"No." I climb out of the truck. Walking around it quickly, I pull her door open. Leaning over her, I release her seat belt. "I need you."

I press a quick kiss to Charlotte's mouth. Shock and surprise fill her face.

I raise a brow in question. Charlotte grins, shuffling to the edge of the seat. Raising her arms, she silently asks me to help her down.

I laugh, the sound still foreign to me, but I happily tuck my hands under her ass and lift her from my truck.

I don't release her, though. Instead, I carry her across the yard to the men's restroom, kicking the door open.

Duke walks out of the main building, probably thinking I want gas pumped. When he sees Charlotte in my arms, the old man grins.

I pause in the bathroom doorway. Duke points at the pump and then at my vehicle.

I shake my head and nod down to Charlotte and then into the bathroom. Duke throws his head back and laughs, waving a hand at me as if to say have at it.

Charlotte buries her face in my chest, smothering her laughter with my shirt.

I like that she's embarrassed. It's cute. I love that she seeks comfort from me like I am the only one in the world who can protect her.

I press a kiss to the top of her head as we cross the threshold.

My cock aches, but this is about her. After taking her punishment so well last night and the way she lied at the police station today, taking care of her is the least I can do.

I push away the anger at my plans being thwarted earlier by that dick Cooper thinking he can manipulate Samantha into giving him what he wants.

A lesson I am sure she is still feeling. Kaleb was almost as pissed as I was.

Almost.

Once inside, I waste no time pressing Charlotte against the bathroom door. My mouth attaches to hers, showing her how much I want this and how much I appreciate what she just did.

She lets out a startled yelp when I hoist her higher until she finds herself with her thighs thrown over my shoulders, her dress shoved to her waist, and my face in her snatch.

Greedily, I eat. Her hands grip my hair as my tongue thrusts inside her over and over. I might just keep this no panties rule, seeing as no bras has worked out so well so far.

I devour every inch of her until she screams out in release. Her pleasure-drugged smile greets me when I come up for air, only to transform into an *O* when I start all over again.

CHAPTER THIRTY

Charlie

Warm water soothes my body, my thighs widening on their own as the heat seeps in.

The tub is large, but Daniel is larger. His big frame sits behind me, his legs barely fitting inside the porcelain.

Everyone was happy to see us when we came back, his dad saying how he looked forward to having all his family together under one roof for a few more days. Helen was quick to point out that that now included me.

My eyes fill at the memory. I have a big family back home in Ohio, one that I have missed seeing every day since moving to college, so the thought of having another here fills my heart.

Daniel presses a kiss to the side of my head, and I

realize that I let out another sigh. Patiently, he waits for me to talk.

"Will I ever get to see my family again?" I whisper.

When he doesn't answer, I peer up at him over my shoulder.

"You can come with me." I turn back around, resting my back against his chest. "Ohio's not too far."

Another kiss on my wet hair is my only answer before Daniel asks me his own question. Well, not exactly asks. A question suggests I have an option to respond when he and I both know I don't.

"Tell me about them, your family." His hands massage over my arms, washing the soap away. His fingers are strong and steady as they move over me.

My chest rises on an unsteady breath as thoughts of not seeing them again close in on the edges of my brain. "I lived with my mom and grandma before college," I explain, peeking back at him. "My dad died a few months after I was born, from a heart attack. Went to work one day and just never came home." My words taper off quietly, my shoulder slumping under his hands. "My mom never recovered," I tell him.

Daniel stays quiet behind me, but even in the silence, I can feel the strength he's trying to give me. "I'm an only child," I whisper. "After my dad, my mom wouldn't even look at another man. Said she'd had her one true love and that he gave her me. I was all she needed." The memory of us cuddling on the sofa and looking at pictures of the man we both miss dearly chokes me, my words lodging in the back of my throat.

Sniffling, I wipe at my blurry eyes. "It was okay, though. It's hard to stay lonely in a house full of people. My cousins were always there to see Grandma or wanting to play with me." I smile, trying to lessen the worry rolling off him. I sigh wistfully. "I'm glad Mom got to love my dad the way she did, but I wish I had a sibling. I envy the relationship you have with Michael. That man loves you more than himself." A laugh rips out of me. "He'd literally do anything to protect you, even kill me to save you from yourself."

Daniel's whole body turns to stone behind me. "He said that? Those words?" His sharp tone cuts through me.

Shit. I don't want to answer, but I want to leave him waiting even less. "Yes," I croak. "But he was just thinking of you. I'm okay," I reassure him.

The temperature in the room drops, and it's not from the steadily cooling bath water. I reach out and rub his knee, squeezing it in a way I hope conveys that I'm okay with Michael's words, that I understand them.

The man is willing to take something away, to make a call no one else will in order to protect his brother. Who wouldn't understand and respect that?

Daniel's hand joins mine, our fingers interlacing over the skin of his thigh where he settles them. "You have two brothers and a sister now." I feel the weight of his words sink in just as he adds, "You won't ever be alone again, Charlotte." Our chests rise and fall in sync as we just breathe, resting and relaxing away from the world, hiding in our own bubble.

"When did you first kill?" The question slips out into the quiet room, disturbing the peaceful energy.

At first, I don't think he'll answer. His hand dips into the water pooled at my hips, soaking the sponge in his hand. Raising it, he pours water over my chest, ripples of water wash over my skin.

"When I was eighteen."

I wait for him to continue, but he doesn't. Soaping his hands, he rubs my shoulders with firm hands as he washes me.

Images of Daniel as a young boy float about my head, but after what I witnessed on Friday, I cannot imagine such a young man doing something so evil, not even him. "Why?"

"They deserved it."

Again, Daniel doesn't elaborate. My brow furrows, and my shoulders sag under his hands.

"Our parents," he tells me, kissing the nape of my neck, "the ones before Helen and Christopher, they weren't kind or loving. Our father would drink, get mean, and beat the shit out of whoever made the most noise."

I swallow my response, not wanting to interrupt in fear of him stopping.

"One night, Michael cried too much. He was

scared. Our father came for him in the night, but I was waiting. I was big, even then." His hands gently wash me as he speaks, as if he can wash the words away with the soap. "I taunted him, egged him on. Said things I knew would make him forget about Michael. And he did."

My tears roll out, hiding in the water dripping down from my hair.

"But it didn't matter how big I was or how much I wanted to protect Michael. He was a forty-three-year-old grown man. I didn't stand a chance."

I lace my fingers with his and raise our hands to my chest, letting him feel the way my heart beats for him.

"He beat me so bad that my mother thought I was dead. I had a broken jaw, a fractured skull."

Now I know why Michael would do anything for Daniel. He deserves it. His past actions demand loyalty.

"I don't remember most of the beating, just the pain and his angry yells of what he would do to Michael if I ever talked back again."

My mouth feels bone-dry, and sobs shake my chest. Who would do that to a child? Any child.

"It was a while before I could speak again anyway, but by the time I could, I found I didn't want to. Michael accepted that and so did the Cromwells, our new family." I can hear the smile in his voice. "Kaleb's birth mother was a whore from a few towns over. She didn't know who his father was and had no interest in feeding another mouth. They took him in a few years after us, but he's not adopted. They couldn't without his mother's permission."

Daniel's fingers flex under mine.

"You're a part of this family now." Those words turn me on, or maybe it's the way his tongue traces the shell of my ear.

Either way, I let the sensations roll over me and push my hips back into his.

Our exploits don't go too far before shouting from downstairs penetrates our haze, and angry voices float up. Daniel is quick to react. Jumping from the bath, he rushes out ready to defend his family.

The thought shouldn't make me clench the way that it does, shouldn't make my heart ache for him. It shouldn't make me love him more.

CHAPTER THIRTY-ONE

Charlie

I thought it, and now I can't take the words back, at least from myself. No one else has to know.

I love him.

I love the man who helped to kill my friends.

Fucking useless, I can't even fall in love right.

The shouting continues, so I hurry out of the bath, drying off quickly, and head downstairs. After all, this was my family to protect too now, right?

By the time I make it downstairs, Kaleb holds Daniel against the wall while Michael talks to him quietly. His hushed tones don't carry over to where I stand on the stairs, but it's clear to everyone that his words are not working.

Christopher is arguing with Officer Cooper by the

door, so I head over to Daniel to see what is wrong. Maybe they didn't believe my story.

Before I can reach them, someone grabs my arm. Their grip is tight and painful. Another officer pulls me to the door.

"No!" I try to shake him off.

My shout gets everyone's attention, and all hell breaks loose.

Daniel rips away from his brothers, running toward me.

"Freeze, asshole," Officer Copper yells, drawing his weapon.

"No!" I scream when Daniel grabs an ornament off the mantel. They'll kill him.

Pulling with everything I have, I rip myself away from the officer and run to Daniel. His arms wrap around me tight, like I might disappear.

"You heard my son. Charlie's not going anywhere. She's a Cromwell now. I'll have your fucking job for this."

My heart swells at Christopher's words.

"I have an order signed by a judge that says she's coming with me," Cooper says smugly.

Daniel tries to move around me, and fear grips me at what could happen.

"Anyone who tries to stop me will be arrested or shot and not in that order." Cooper's arrogant tone only serves to rile everyone more.

"Please, Daniel, don't. I won't ever see you again if you kill them," I plead in a hushed tone.

He blinks down at me.

"They'll lock you up."

"I want to speak to McCallister right now," Michael demands.

"He's away. Had to rush out of town for a family emergency," the other officer explains.

"Where are you taking her?" Helen asks.

"Somewhere tomorrow that's not your business, somewhere I can speak to her away from you and your boys. This is a witness protection order," Cooper gloats.

"And tonight, it's already eight in the evening?" Christopher tuts.

Clearly not used to being questioned, Cooper snaps, "I'll find somewhere."

Christopher accepts the challenge. "I want to see that order. I'm calling the judge right now."

"Call whoever you want, but Charlie comes with me right now, or you're all coming to lock up, and then no one's calling anyone."

He's right. They need to be free to sort this out. I need to go.

"Daniel," Michael warns.

"I'll come for you." The promise is whispered in my ear.

I nod, framing his face, our eyes locked. Stretching up onto my tiptoes, I press a kiss to his mouth.

His hands tighten on my hips, once, then twice, before his touch reluctantly falls away.

I look around at the family in the room, each one

wearing a different expression of anger, worry, hurt. Not wanting to make things worse, I put on a brave face and follow Officer Cooper out of the cabin.

CHAPTER THIRTY-TWO

Daniel

"Ahhh," I roar, sweeping the tools off the side bench.

My chest heaves, but no matter how hard I try to draw in air, it feels like I can't breathe.

I have never felt this kind of rage, not even when we were kids.

A hand touches my back, and I quickly shrug it off, but it just returns a few seconds later.

"Michael," I warn. He means well, but I am not in the right headspace. I can't think. Charlotte took my thoughts with her. My mind feels foggy.

"We'll get her back."

"Do you even want to?" I challenge.

Michael looks stunned by my words. "You love her, so of course I want her back. You being happy means more than anything to me, Daniel. I would do anything for you."

"So I've heard," I snap.

Recognition washes over his face. "I would never hurt her. I just wanted to scare her." He shrugs sheepishly.

"She's not yours to scare," I reprimand.

"No," he agrees, "but you want to keep her, and I want to keep you." Michael swallows hard, and I give him a second to find the right words. "I need you, Daniel. Charlie is scared of you, but she's seen your heart." My brother blinks back tears. "If her thinking that I don't have one is what it takes to keep you safe and happy, I'm okay with that."

My chest twists at his words; my love for him consumes me. But I need him to know that it can't happen again.

"It stops now. Please don't make me choose, Mikey."

He nods, his tears escaping at his childhood nick-name, and suddenly, all I see is a seven-year-old boy who needs to be protected again.

"We both know you wouldn't live with yourself, either way," Michael whispers, knowing that I am unable to choose between the two people who I love the most. He wipes at his cheeks and chuckles. "Look what women do to us?"

I laugh with him because who the fuck would have thought we could ever say those words.

"We'll get her back, Daniel."

I know.

"Cooper blindsided us, but he's desperate and running out of time. Dad is on the phone with anyone who'll answer," he tells me, motioning to where the main house is, beyond the walls. "He'll want to put distance between the two of you tonight, but he'll need to sleep."

I nod to show I'm listening. And I am, I'm hanging on to every word. Michael is thinking logically when I can't.

"Go find her. Make tonight count because after today, you'll need to wait until we can get this sorted out with the judge. You don't want them to take her away because you lost focus. Keep control now, and you can have forever with her."

He's right. I know he is, but my whole body is on edge.

I need her. I need to lose myself in her. I need to feel her body against mine, to know that we are one, that we can win. That she's still mine.

CHAPTER THIRTY-THREE

Charlie

I sit in silence, ignoring Officer Fuckface, scowling at him whenever he has the nerve to talk to me.

"Listen, kid."

Kid? He's like thirty, tops. *Prick.*

Clearly unable to read the room, he continues unfazed by me ignoring him.

"I know you're afraid of them boys, but I'm going to keep you safe."

I scoff. He clearly has no idea who he's dealing with. Daniel would crush him.

My eyes grow heavy, having been in the car for hours already.

"There's a motel up ahead. We'll stay there tonight and continue in the morning."

"Where?" I ask, annoyed that I have to speak to him but wanting to know where he's taking me.

"Back to your college. I figure it's far enough away that by the time the Cromwells figure it out, you'll have told me everything."

I perk up at the news.

We pull into a typical-looking roadside motel. The sign flashes blue, the M staying dark.

I follow him blindly up the stairs, the wood creaking under my feet.

"You better have gotten two rooms," I spit at him, glaring at his back. I know he did since I was in the office when he paid, but I feel the need to poke at him.

The dick raises his hand and jiggles two sets of keys.

"No making calls, no leaving. Don't think I won't arrest you if you even think about it," he warns, opening the door. "I mean it, Charlie. I'll throw you in jail along with your little boyfriend."

I nod, stepping into the room. I close the door harshly when he tries to follow me in, but his foot blocks the frame.

"I need to check the room."

"I think it's safe unless some serial killer managed to guess which room I'd be in during the time it took you to barter for the cheapest rooms, of which you get the only double bed." Yeah, asshat, I was paying attention.

Chastised, Cooper removes his foot, and I firmly

close the door, sliding the lock in place and feeling like I can finally breathe for the first time in five hours.

I brace myself against the door and pray that the Cromwells have enough power to sort this out before it's too late.

"Shh," a voice warns.

I open my mouth to scream, but a hand traps the noise before I can let it out, while another hand lays itself over my own, entwining his fingers on the door.

Daniel! How the fuck?

The hand on my mouth moves to my hair. Gripping it, he pulls my head back onto his shoulder stretching my neck, something his mouth takes full advantage of.

I moan.

"Shh, good girl. You have to keep quiet. Can you do that?"

"Yes, sir." I grin.

He tears me away from the door, tossing me onto the twin bed.

I watch, propped on my elbows as Daniel pulls the frame of the bed, the feet scraping the floor as he moves it away from the wall.

A knock instantly sounds on the adjoining wall.

Fuck!

I look at Daniel as if to ask "What now?"

He waves a hand in a circular motion, telling me to deal with it while he pulls the shirt out of his pants.

"I'm okay," I shout. "No serial killers in here, just a wonky bed."

"Remember what I said." Cooper's voice carries through the thin, stained wall.

Daniel eyes the wall like he wants to bash Cooper with the nearest object, and frankly, I don't blame him.

"On your knees, hands on the headboard."

I do as I'm told; I need this just as much as Daniel.

Strong hands tear at my panties, and I have never been so grateful for dresses. The sound of tearing fabric shouts out Daniel's impatience and is my only warning before his thick fingers probe at me.

"How did you know?" I pant. Needing to know how he knew where to find me.

His deep chuckle penetrates my ears just as his cock does my pussy. "With you, I will always know."

His promise hangs between us as he brutally plunges inside my body, over and over.

I bite back my moan, my lips stinging as my teeth pierce the skin.

Pain spreads out from my neck, Daniel's teeth sinking in to hide his own sounds of pleasure.

The room fills with our heavy breathing, the sound of flesh hitting flesh the only clue as to what is happening.

Trying to reach around, I finger the zipper at the back of my dress. Daniel's thrusts turn short as his hand knocks mine away, unfastening me quickly.

I push off the thin sleeves, needing to free my

breasts, the cotton scratching as they move with the power of his body rocking mine.

The bed beneath us groans along with us, and I pray Cooper doesn't hear because I might be the one who kills him if we have to stop before I come.

"Uh, uh." Sharp, powerful thrusts force sounds from deep within me that I cannot control.

Suddenly, my head is shoved forward, and the hand fisting my hair twists as he growls his order right in my ear.

"Come."

And because I am his good girl, I do as I'm told. My scream is silent. My whole body shakes uncontrollably as my pussy pulses over and over, milking him, drawing his own orgasm out of him and into me.

His thrusts don't stop as he fills me over and over.

Together, we stay like that, my head on the bed, my ass high with Daniel buried deep, panting together as we try to catch our breaths.

His hands rub over my hips, my body rocking when he occasionally withdraws and pushes back in.

He's still coming!

The realization sets off another orgasm for me, and his chuckle fills the room as he feels it roll over his deeply buried cock.

"You'll always be mine."

CHAPTER THIRTY-FOUR

Charlie

Last night was the best sex in my so far short sex life, frantic and emotional. I may not have much experience, but I know not many people get to achieve that kind of high too many times in their lives.

Which is why waking up alone, with only my sore, used pussy and cum-dried thighs as evidence, hurt even more.

So here I sit, feeling sad and used in the passenger seat of Officer Fuckface's car outside of my college without panties on because apparently today didn't start off bad enough, while Officer Cooper gets yelled at by his boss, Cromwell's local sheriff, so loudly that I can hear his words from here. Who apparently is not happy about his subordinate going behind his back while he was out of town.

"You lied about having evidence of them being there! You told Judge Gregson she was a willing witness who had been kidnapped!"

"Sir!"

"Don't you sir me. Get your ass back here. The only one who's kidnapped that girl is you!"

I curl my lips inward, trying not to smirk.

"We have a video of a masked man entering the front bedroom, evidence that the Cromwells gave us from a security camera at the front of the camp. One masked man, so your theory of all three brothers doing it doesn't even work!"

I fidget in my seat.

"Say, yes sir and get back here. Clean out your desk."

"Yes, sir." His tone is sad and dejected. It pulls at my heart but only a little.

"Oh, and Cooper, I suggest you tell Miss Ramsey about the temporary restraining order you filed. Perhaps it's best she stays away from Cromwell Town until the family can sort that out and get it dismissed."

"What?" I demand.

Cooper scratches at his red ear, throwing his cell phone onto the dash. "I might have also called the local police here. If any of the Cromwells show up, they'll be arrested."

I stare at him open-mouthed; he can't be serious.

"They did it. We both know it," he snaps.

I don't speak, just stare at him through tear-filled eyes.

Together, we climb out of his squad car.

"I don't care what they say. Do yourself a favor, Charlie, and stay away from Cromwell Town and the family that runs it for good. I'll be watching them closely," he tells me. "Don't fool yourself. He's not capable of love. None of them are. He's not coming back for you."

When I only continue to glare, Cooper adds, "Not that he could, even if he wanted to."

I blink at him, not sure how to respond, as the wind wraps around me and makes me shiver.

"If I see you again, I'll go after the whole family, not just him. I'll start with Michael." His parting words ring over in my head as I walk toward my dorm. My heart breaks with each step I take. I love Daniel and would never risk his freedom, but Michael means the world to him, and I would risk his family even less.

Walking into the dorm without Amy and Laura is awful. My heart squeezes at the sight of the stuffed orange cat perched on Laura's pillows, waiting for her to come home and cuddle it. My stomach has knots, knowing she isn't coming home. None of them are.

I drop my bag at the foot of my bed and slump onto the edge of the mattress. The soreness between my legs as I sit is a reminder of last night. Of what I did with Daniel, what I have continuously done with him since Friday night.

Disgust rolls through me. Sitting among their belongings surrounded by memories, I'm disappointed he left, that Daniel didn't make me stay.

I shove off the bed in anger and dump out my bag. Clothes, toiletries, and my camera tumble out onto the pale-pink duvet.

Reaching out, I grab the digital camera and press the power button to bring it to life. The screen flicks on quickly, and I find my finger moving to the arrowed button that brings my photos to view without thinking of it. My face along with Amy's and Laura's smile back at me, huddled close in the dark main room of the cabin; it was the last photo I took Friday night.

My throat closes at the memory of what came only a few hours later, images run behind my closed eyelids. I don't need photos of that. I will never forget, no matter how much I try.

I suck in a shaky breath and press the back button, turning to the next photo, and the next, and the next until I'm back to the first image. All twelve photographs stab at me, one by one, each more painful than the last.

The photos keep revolving, my finger pressing without my permission, my eyes search each image as if I could bring them to life if I look hard enough.

I'm on the fourth image for probably the eighth time when my eyes catch something in the background. I zoom in past the image of myself smiling at the camera and close in on the trees.

Holy fuck.

There's something in the woods behind me, someone.

Daniel.

Crouched next to a tree, he blends in with the forest floor, his camouflage clothing making it almost impossible for me to find him, almost.

I zoom out a little. I don't need to go far before I find who I'm looking for. Both Michael and Kaleb are close by.

Had they watched us all day? Stalked us before coming to the camp that night? Should I tell someone?

I'm confused. My heart and my head are at war, and neither was coming out on top, but both were left bloody and bruised by the time I can tear myself away from the camera.

I need to get away—away from this room, away from that camera, and away from deciding what the right thing to do is.

Quickly, I grab the clothes hamper, shoving everything I took on the trip in, even those that didn't get worn.

I lock all thoughts of Daniel and his family in my dorm room along with the camera when I lock the door. Quickening my steps, I keep my head dropped low and don't stop until I'm at the campus laundry.

Having done this a thousand times, I move on autopilot, my brain happy for my body to take over.

I don't think about Daniel again until I'm tucked up in bed later that night, the room as dark as my soul. My face is wet with tears as I stare at the screen on my camera. The war is still going on inside me.

I've gone over these images dozens of times in the past few hours, seeking out the face of the man who turned my world upside down.

He's in two of them.

Behind me, always hidden and always watching. Like he knew what Dale would try to do. *Like he was looking out for me.*

That thought makes me do it. My breath stops as I press the trash icon. In a trance, I stare as if it is someone else doing it, their finger making all of the images disappear.

Memory card empty. I blink at the blurry words.

No one else is here. I did this. I just deleted the evidence. I deleted my friends' faces.

Turning, I place the camera onto the small nightstand. The first sob is followed by the next quickly, and before I know it, I'm sucking in air, trying not to choke on my grief and loss. But mostly, I cry for what I don't have . . . regret.

"You can say anything here, Charlotte. This is a safe place."

My fingers twitch at the name, but I don't have the energy to correct him. I don't have the energy for anything.

The past few days have blended into one giant blur of trying to keep one foot in front of the other.

I haven't told anyone about the photos or what I did. I don't think even Michael could pry that information out of me, so this calm, cherry-eating fuckface is definitely not getting it out of me.

I pinch the bridge of my nose at the name my mind has conjured for the college-appointed counselor.

Kaleb would be proud.

My heart squeezes. The deleted images aren't the only thing I won't be speaking of.

I stare blankly back at the counselor because I have nothing to say. They'd have to waterboard the details of last weekend out of me because I'm certainly not cracking when he tells me I'm safe.

"Okay." He nods, sensing that today will go the same as our other sessions. "Just know that when you're ready, I'm right here." He ducks down to catch my eye.

I blink quickly at the sincerity in his blue eyes and give him a grateful nod. He's just trying to do his job, and I appreciate that, but no one can help me right now, at least no one that's here.

Satisfied, he gives me a small smile. "I'll write you another note, but feel free to go to class if you feel like it." He winks.

* * *

I stare up at the outside of the building. The campus feels different. Empty, like me.

My room is even worse. I hate coming back here every day. I step into the room and see Amy's and Laura's empty desks and stripped beds. Someone has been in here to empty their things while I was out skipping class. Like my best friends were never here.

Pain pierces my chest; my friends are gone, and that fact has never been more striking.

A sob wracks my whole body. I let my sorrow drag me to the ground, and I crumple where I stand.

I can't stay here any longer. It's only been three days, and I can't take it much more. I need to go home.

I'm still crying when my mom answers my call.

"Hey, baby," she says cheerfully down the line.

I can't speak through my sobs.

"Charlie, oh baby. Please don't cry."

I try to calm myself and take comfort in the fact that I'm talking to my mom, but it's not enough.

"What do you mean, she's crying? Give me the phone. Let me speak to her." I hear my grandmother demand over the line.

"Charlie, you there?" My mom must have given her the phone. "Press a button if you can hear me, sweetheart."

I do as I'm told.

"Good girl," she tells me. The words only serve to

make me cry more. Everything that I did with Daniel seems so much worse now that I sit in the dorm room that I shared with Amy and Laura.

"Sweetheart, your mother is leaving right now. She's going to come fetch you. I knew we shouldn't have listened when you said you were okay." I get lost in her words. I sit on the floor of my dorm and wait for my mom to come take me home.

Maybe there, I won't feel the guilt so bad.

Maybe there, I won't question why he hasn't come for me.

Maybe there, I won't miss him so much.

I wake slowly, the feeling of fingers combing through my hair pulls me into consciousness.

"I have to go to work, baby."

"Hmm," I hum, showing my mom I heard her, too sleepy to say words.

She sighs above me. "Try to get out of the house today, okay? I know it's tough. Maybe take your grandma to that new food place in town or Christmas shopping?"

"Maybe," I whisper, but we both know it's a lie.

I cuddle Mr. Bear, my childhood stuffed animal, a little closer. He doesn't judge me, and he keeps my secrets, too, which is why he's the only one in a house full of family that I whispered my suspicions to.

"Jessie, leave my grandbaby alone."

I don't even need to look back at them to know both have an identical pinched expression on their faces. "It's been three weeks, Mom. I need her to eat more, or I'm calling the doctor again."

I can't put it off any longer. I need to know.

Grabbing my sneakers from beside my bedroom door, I shove my feet into them, barely taking the time to lace them.

I fist the car keys as I slam the door closed. My hand shakes so hard it takes a few times to insert the key.

Unfortunately, the local Costco is humming with people, and by the time I get to the checkout, my nerves are shot.

A woman in her mid-twenties stands in line before me with a small boy throwing a tantrum at her feet. I feel my panic grow and clutch my one item even tighter.

After what feels far too long for a line of just two people to be served, where the universe is cruelly tormenting me, the cashier finally hands me my change.

Speed walking to the back of the store, I beeline for the bathroom, not wanting to wait until I get home.

An employee opens his mouth as I rush past him, and I glare through my tears, daring him to stop me.

Now is not the time to fuck with me.

I breathe a sigh of relief when I see the ladies' room is empty. Rushing into the stall, I sit staring at the test in my hands.

It takes a few minutes as I apparently do not pee well under pressure, and I have to remind myself to calm down. Nothing has happened yet.

I could be wrong.

I place the used test on the counter as I wash my hands. Gripping the side, I stare at myself in the mirror. The dark circles under my eyes are a testament to how I have not been sleeping. I look gaunt and pale.

These past three weeks have been hell. I can't eat; I can't sleep. And I think the reason for both is him.

I hang my head, unable to look at myself any longer.

Three minutes, it's time.

I drag in a deep breath and open my eyes.

Positive.

I'm pregnant.

Fuck, fuck, fuck.

I almost swallow my tongue in shock when I see a large hand slide around my waist, settling on my stomach.

"Mine." The word is growled into my ear, full of possession and pride, and I know he's not talking about just me anymore.

I know he will never let us go.

I peek to see our reflection; his gaze is fixed on the

two pink lines that have appeared on the white stick sitting in front of us.

My hand joins his resting above where our child grows inside me. His hand rises and falls with my rapid breaths.

Slowly, my breathing settles, and my panic leaves.

He's here. He came for me, for us.

Tears drop, one by one as I blink.

Guiding our hands, I move them until his fingers reach the top of my pants before easing them inside.

I watch the slight lift at the corner of his mouth, and I know that he knows my other secret.

He knows that I don't want him to let us go.

EPILOGUE

Charlie

My family loves him. Well, my grandmother does. His stern silence and masculine energy remind her of my grandpa, and really, her approval is all he needs to win over the whole family.

I smile at my grandmother, waving from my seat inside the truck.

My cheeks flush, sad at the thought of never coming back.

"Thirty hours, that's how far Ohio is. Less than four if we fly," Daniel tells me. Our eyes lock as the meaning sinks in. We can come back.

I can have both.

The light, warmth, and chaos of my family, as well as the love, darkness, and loyalty of Daniel and his family.

The best of both worlds.
What more could I ask for?

THE END.

ABOUT THE AUTHOR

Jennifer Ivy is an author that loves to write dark romance.

Her debut novel, Mine, is the first book in A Killer's Love Series.

The author can be found on several social media sites, such as:

Instagram; jenniferivy_author

TikTok; jenniferivy_author

Goodreads; Jennifer Ivy

Printed in Great Britain
by Amazon